*A Delicately
Personal Matter*

Also by Richard R. Werry

CASKET FOR A LYING LADY
HAMMER ME HOME
WHERE TOWN BEGINS

A Delicately Personal Matter

A J. D. Mulroy Mystery Novel

Richard R. Werry

Dodd, Mead & Company • New York

No part of this book may be reproduced in any form
without permission in writing from the publisher.
Published by Dodd, Mead & Company, Inc.
79 Madison Avenue, New York, N.Y. 10016
Distributed in Canada by
McClelland and Stewart Limited, Toronto
Manufactured in the United States of America

First Edition

Library of Congress Cataloging-in-Publication Data

Werry, Richard R.
  A delicately personal matter.

  I. Title.
PS3545.E8254D44   1986   813'.54   86-6332
ISBN 0-396-08851-1

1 2 3 4 5 6 7 8 9 10

For Marvelous Martie

1

"A delicately personal matter" read her letter, which I found waiting for me when I returned from Florida a bit bruised but much wealthier than when I had left. The Winkle affair had drawn me to Florida during Michigan's most glorious season, late fall, when half the population of Birmingham seemed to be "up north" closing cottages, storing boats for the winter, and incidentally taking thousands of color photos of the mingling of oak, maple, birch, and poplar leaves contrasted with spires of green firs.

"If you move the camera just a smidgen as you shoot," my would-be husband and sometimes lover-lawyer Ed Rogers told me once, "you can get an effect as impressionistic as anything Turner ever painted!"

"There's a difference," I suggested, but did not pursue the distinction.

Now fall was definitely finished. A northwest wind whined at the windows of my apartment and office, there wasn't a spot of blue in the overcast that was sky, and the twenty-five-degree temperature read eight on the TV wind-chill thermometer.

Mrs. Everett Wilkinson had written in a firm hand that was half-printing, on a plain sheet of good bond paper, and had given only a phone number by which to contact her. There was no return address on the envelope. This did not particularly surprise me. When people employ me, they usually are close to despair or desperation: they want something back that they have lost—more often through foul play than carelessness, but they don't want to reveal their faults or expose themselves to ridicule or danger. I am more often than not a last resort, but until they decide to trust me, they prefer to tell me nothing about themselves. Of course, I had consulted all the metropolitan telephone directories. There must have been two hundred Wilkinsons in the area. But there was no way I could check which one represented her husband because I didn't know his first name.

The voice that answered my ring was obviously that of a servant.

"Hello," it intoned in a long practiced singsong.

"Mrs. Everett Wilkinson, please," I replied.

"May I inquire who is calling?"

"You may. Tell her it's Jane Mulroy calling as she requested me to do."

It had been over a week since the letter arrived, so I thought it might be prudent to remind her that she had written to me just in case she might have found someone else to handle her delicate matter. She needed no reminder.

"Where can we meet?" she asked in a low tense voice.

"I can come see you at your convenience."

"No, not here," she half-whispered. "A restaurant. Any restaurant."

"Do you know where Moffat's is?"

"Oh, yes. When?"

"Name a time and I'll be there."

"This afternoon then. Four o'clock."

"Fine."

"How will I find you?"

"Ask Susan, the hostess, to take you to the library booth in the balcony. She'll understand."

Moffat's is my conference center when it is inconvenient or indiscreet to use my office home on the

2

third floor of the seven-story high-rise three blocks south of the city's main intersection (where Andy Moffat converted his grandfather's huge red barn into Birmingham's most successful, as well as most reasonable, restaurant). I believe the restaurant is Andy's gift to the community, which has made him several times a millionaire by paying exorbitant prices for the land his Scotch farmer forebears bequeathed him in the course of several generations. One of his best friends is my sometimes partner, Ahmad Dakar, ex–University of Michigan and Miami Dolphins tight end, karate instructor, and consumer of Jack Daniel's Manhattans. Andy, ex–World War II marine, six feet five inches tall with a ruddy Scotch face beneath curly, almost-white hair, and Ahmad, also ex-marine, six eight and very black, make quite a spectacle strolling among the shrunken old widows who sip cocktails before having their five o'clock dinner. For that matter, Ahmad and Andy dwarf most of the businessmen and attorneys who crowd about the long bar for the daily ritual pickup drink or two or four to be consumed at all costs between leaving the office and going home to the wife and dinner.

I arrived promptly two minutes before four, and Susan, the afternoon hostess, pointed upward to the balcony before I could even say hello. I don't know what kind of woman I expected Mrs. Wilkinson to be— I don't recall that I had any proper expectations at all—but I certainly did not expect her to be the commanding presence she turned out to be. In the first place, she was half a foot taller than my five feet five inches, I would guess forty pounds heavier than my 123 pounds, and at least twenty years my senior. Yet despite her fifty years, the only sign of aging about her was the more gray than brown hair, which she wore in what years ago used to be called a pageboy bob. Her skin was as smooth as mine, her body as firm as a professional tennis player's. She wore a custom-tailored gray suit, mildly striped, which nearly matched the more gray than blue color of her eyes.

An executive of some sort, I speculated, as I slid into the booth facing her after introducing myself, then rejected this notion not because her fingernails were as short as the average man's but because of the traces of red dye lining several quicks. An artist of some sort—graphics, perhaps?—I wondered, but thought better of this conclusion at once. Mrs. Wilkinson was too "gotten together" to be any kind of artist, too much in control of all she surveyed.

"I know I need hardly say that this interview is to be held in the strictest confidence, Miss Mulroy," she began, leaning forward toward me across the table so that she need not raise her voice.

"Of course," I replied, trying to identify the scent that the air circulator in the smoke-eater above us wafted toward me. It was not a perfume exactly, yet a familiar scent.

"I don't want anyone to know that I've hired you. Is that clear?"

"You haven't hired me yet, Mrs. Wilkinson," I said. What was that scent?

"And whether you do hire me or not will depend on the nature of the job you wish me to undertake. I must tell you at once that I do not involve myself in marital disputes or spy on spouses suspected of infidelity. If that is the nature of your delicately personal matter, I can recommend a man who will work for you, but I will not."

A faint smile glided across her lips, but faded almost before it had formed.

"I'm quite aware of the kind of work you do and don't do, Miss Mulroy, and I hope you will undertake to help me. I don't know what kind of fee you may charge, but if it is not wildly exorbitant, I am prepared to pay your rates."

I think it was at this moment that I recognized the scent.

"Who referred you to me?" I asked.

"I'd rather not say," she answered, "but I trust his judgment completely."

Gail, the east balcony afternoon waitress, appeared bearing one up-Margarita on her tray.

"Compliments of Mr. Dakar," she said, setting it down in front of me, "and he'd be happy to buy your friend a drink."

She turned toward Mrs. Wilkinson, who looked more annoyed than pleased by the interruption.

"A white wine spritzer will do," she said brusquely, and as Gail trotted off, added, "You appear to be well known here."

"It's my office away from my office, Doctor. I understand a good many of your colleagues have similar relaxing oases though usually they're in private clubs inaccessible to the general public."

She was startled, and I knew that my scent-recognition had been correct.

"How did you know?"

"Merthiolate traces on the fingernails of your right hand, and cologne of alcohol and strong soap."

I could have added prescription-authority syndrome but saw nothing to be gained by antagonizing her. Gail returned with a white wine spritzer, and the doctor, after she took a sip, smiled.

"I seem to have gotten off on the wrong foot, don't I?"

"Do you treat a patient who won't tell you his symptoms?"

"By the time they get to me, Miss Mulroy, I have a complete medical diagnosis of their disease. I'm an oncologist."

"Tumors."

"Right. Most of them malignant. You know, I had hoped to keep my identity secret from you, but I realize now that's impractical. You wouldn't accept me on that basis, would you?"

"Dr. Wilkinson—is it really Wilkinson?"

"No. I'm Dr. Elizabeth Mansfield, and I direct the Beaumont Hospital Oncological Clinic. Now, can we start over?"

"Then that wasn't a maid who answered my telephone call but a hospital receptionist?"

"It was my secretary, and you called my private office number. I had told her you might call and ask for a Mrs. Wilkinson."

"Didn't she think that a little strange?"

"She's been with me for years and is used to the games some patients will play to conceal from their families or friends the fact that they are, or may soon be, under treatment for cancer. She never asks questions."

"The ideal secretary. Well, let's start over, Doctor, unless you would like to discuss my fee before you discuss your problem. It's quite simple, really. I charge one hundred and fifty dollars a day plus whatever expenses the job may incur, plus ten percent of the marketable value of whatever I may recover for you. With money or securities, of course, the value is easy to estimate. But with jewelry there's often a problem, and I resolve it by insisting upon appraisals by two reputable jewelers, one of whom I will select, the other to be selected by the client. Do you agree to this arrangement?"

Once again Dr. Mansfield's lips suggested a smile.

"To the daily charge and expenses, yes. But I'm afraid we'll have to substitute ministers, or priests if you prefer, for the jewelers because what I want you to recover might best be described as my brother-in-law's soul. Let me explain."

The gist of what Dr. Mansfield told me follows, without the interruptions of my questions and other asides irrelevant to her story. For example, a second spritzer for the doctor and a second Margarita for me.

Elizabeth Mansfield's sister Charlotte was eleven years younger than she, a surprise baby to a mother of forty-four years. At fifty the mother died of breast cancer that had not been controlled after a partial mastectomy. In the course of the ensuing years, while she was going to college and medical school at the University of Pittsburgh, the city of her birth, Elizabeth became surrogate parent to her sister Charlotte, as their father, a structural stress engineer for a large contracting company, traveled from one assignment to another, often as far away as Saudi Arabia. Charlotte brought all her childish and later her adolescent problems to Elizabeth until, in her junior year of college at Wayne State University, where she had enrolled to be near Elizabeth, she met and subsequently married Emmett Harvey, an enterprising young stockbroker. In time, she produced three children at intervals of two years, moved into a four-bedroom, two-and-a-half-bath house in a new development in Troy (the most rapidly grow-ing city in the metropolitan Detroit area), where up-wardly mobile young couples were clustering on their way, thcy hoped, to better homes in Birmingham or Bloomfield Hills.

Charlotte, married, seemed totally happy, devoted to her husband and children, and dutifully invited her older sister to Sunday dinner once or twice a month. For years she had had no need of advice other than medical from her older sister, and Elizabeth was utterly surprised when six weeks ago Charlotte, tense to the point of tears, confided the difficulties that appeared to have destroyed what had been her very successful marriage.

As if he had suffered a concussion, Emmett had suddenly become distant, distrait even. He no longer seemed to enjoy playing with or instructing his children. He "could not or would not respond to Charlotte's connubial advances," as Dr. Mansfield delicately put it. He began to stay out until midnight or later, rarely eating dinner at home, pleading the press of business. He never initiated conversation with Charlotte and responded monosyllabically to her attempts to draw him out; he became sullen, even morose, if she persisted. It was a side of him Charlotte had never before encountered, and she was baffled and distraught. Of course, at first she suspected another woman, but there was no evidence of one—no strange phone calls, no lipstick stains or stray hairs on his clothes, and he was always where he said he would be—at the office as a rule—when Charlotte telephoned him, whether at noon or midnight.

Has he seen his doctor lately, Elizabeth asked Charlotte. Perhaps he's ill and doesn't want you to know about it. Charlotte didn't know, so Elizabeth telephoned Dr. Brady, the Harveys' internist, explained that Emmett had been acting strangely of late, and inquired whether he could stretch ethics far enough to tell her whether Emmett had visited him lately. He's overdue for a checkup, Dr. Brady said. It had been over two years since he had come to the office. "So now Charlotte doesn't know what to think or do. For that matter, neither do I, short of confronting Emmett and demanding an explanation in the role of mother superior, or the children's godmother," Dr. Mansfield concluded her story.

"I don't get involved in domestic squabbles, Doctor," I said. "But if your assumptions are all correct, or rather your sister's, the problem must originate outside of the home. This is what you believe, is it?"

"I'm sure of it, Miss Mulroy."

"Call me Jane, please."

"I'm sure of it. You have to know Emmett to realize that he isn't the kind of man who would cheat on his wife and children. Let me tell you a little bit about him and you'll understand. He was an unwanted baby whose mother didn't even know who his father was, apparently didn't much care, for that matter. When he was three, she deserted him, leaving him with the landlady of her rooming house with no note of explanation and two weeks in arrears in rent, and she never returned. The landlady turned him over to the county's Children's Aid Society. He moved about from foster home to foster home until he was sixteen, resisting the saccharine attempts of some of his foster mothers to give him affection, which many of them did because he was an extraordinarily handsome teenager. More often than not the husbands, becoming jealous, insisted that he be returned to the Society after a few months' residence. He was a competent student in every subject except math, for which his high school math teachers said he had an unusual aptitude. I suppose it was normal for him to take an interest in computers, and he learned how to program them even before they became a necessity in the world of business.

"Primarily through the sponsorship of his mathematics teachers, he was given a scholarship to Walsh Business College when he graduated from high school—do you know where that is?"

"Just north of Big Beaver Road off Livernois, isn't it?"

"Right. Apparently it's one of the better schools of its kind in the area, and their graduates have little difficulty getting jobs. Emmett went to the accounting office of Merrill, Lynch in Detroit, learned about stocks and bonds, later instructed their local brokerage offices how to use computers to their best advantage, got a license as a broker himself specializing in bond issues, saved his money, even after he married Charlotte, and finally, six years ago, opened his own discount brokerage outlet representing a big Swiss-owned firm."

"I assume that he's fairly well-off then?"

"He's done well, certainly, but the Reagan recession was a tough time for anyone dealing in bonds, I understand."

"Could he be on the verge of bankruptcy, do you think, and has been trying to cope with that problem without worrying Charlotte about it?"

"That's one of the questions I hope you might find the answer to. Dr. Nachwardt, who recommended you to me, seems to think you have sources for determining that sort of thing."

"I'd have to have some specific facts to start with."

"I realize that. If you could get into Emmett's office as an apprentice employee, do you think you could get what you need?"

"Perhaps. But before I say I'll try to help you and your sister, Doctor, I want to have a talk with her. Can you arrange that?"

"I can call her now. The children will be home from school, but I'm sure she'd be glad to meet you here tomorrow sometime."

"Not here. In her home."

"Is that necessary?"

"I prefer it that way, Doctor. You can learn a lot more about animals if you study them in their natural environment rather than in a zoo cage."

"That's not a very pretty thing to say about your favorite restaurant, Jane," Dr. Mansfield remarked, as she slid from the booth to phone her little sister.

2

I am usually amused by the names developers choose for their streets. In the old days, the process was unplanned and rational. The main street of a new settlement, if not called Main Street, probably was given the name of the farmer who owned the field before it was segmented by a road: Bryant Road, or Hutchinson Street. If it had been a wooded area or an orchard cleared for the march of mankind, trees might be remembered by street tags: Cherry Street, Sycamore, Oak. Not any longer. Developers striving for instant tradition rely on English nomenclature: Shrewsbury, York, Westminister, Buckingham adorn the street signs on treeless flats at the edges of American cities, in whole sections of which white flight has left behind a spoor of boarded-up three-layer brick or quarry stone houses. Occasionally, a builder who fancies himself well-read will rely on the names of famous writers: Longfellow, Hawthorne, Whitman Boulevard. I was astounded a couple of years ago to discover the film stars of the Twenties and Thirties memorialized by the street names in a dusty, dry eastern California desert town full of low-priced, veteran-approved, G.I.-loan, asbestos-shingle houses: Harlow Lane, Dressler Drive, Valentino Street.

The developer who had built the three-block-square subdivision in which Charlotte and Emmett Harvey lived was neither pretentious nor literary, but he must have been a ladies' man of broad experience, because all the streets bore women's names: Louisa, Alma, Doreen, Ramona, Victoria. The Harveys lived on Vanessa in the middle of a block of two-story, brick, four-bedroom, two-and-a-half-bath, finished-basement-with-rumpus-room-and-wet-bar houses that looked much larger than they actually were, because the attached two-and-a-half-car brick garage seemed to add an additional four hundred square feet of floor space. Some of the homeowners had endeavored to break the flat monotony of the terrain by replacing the bulldozed maples and oaks with front lawn decorative trees and backyard flowering crab apples or birch clumps. In front of the Harveys' was a young mountain ash still bearing half a dozen orange seed clusters.

Charlotte Harvey evidently had been watching for me, because she had the front door open before I had closed the door of my beige Camaro.

"I'm so glad you could come," she said, as I stepped before her into a ceramic tile hallway. It opened on one side into a living room that had obviously not been decorated by a professional, yet was done in harmonious basic colors. With the clutter of magazines, children's books, and a few child's games on a small end table, the room exuded an air of healthy home life.

"I've a pot of boiling water on the stove, if you'd like some tea."

"Fine."

"Let's go into the kitchen then."

The kitchen with adjoining breakfast nook was done in yellow, and now, facing the west, was flooded with afternoon sunlight. It was a cheerful room with a sliding door leading onto a backyard, where on this not-cold November day I could watch the antics of the family cockatoo on a Mediterranean stone patio.

"I'm having camomile, Miss Mulroy, but I can give you pekoe, green, elderberry, or rose hips if you'd prefer one of those."

12

"Quite an assortment," I said. "The camomile will be fine, I haven't had any for a long time."

"It's good, and good for you, too," Charlotte said. "It settles the stomach, calms the nerves."

No one seeing Dr. Mansfield and Charlotte Harvey side by side would have taken them for sisters. Whereas Elizabeth was tall, solid, square-shouldered, statuesquely handsome, Charlotte was small, slight of structure, delicate as a ceramic doll. Elizabeth was confidently forthright, if not aggressive, but her sister was almost timorous in manner, servile in her desire to please. One could imagine the doctor leading a group of Equal Rights women to protest before the Capitol, but Charlotte looked to be what she was—a woman made to accommodate a man with loving care, and children. Comparing the two while Charlotte made the tea, I experienced a sense of estrangement from my sex. I didn't fit into either category. The Bella Abzugs and Jane Fondas of our time, who bulldozed their way through life screaming at the top of their lungs, knowing full well that no decent man was likely to oppose them physically or demean himself in the eyes of his fellows by screaming back, I considered cheaters, emotional conwomen running a scam as crooked as any carny shell game ever was. On the other hand, I knew I was utterly incapable of subordinating my interests and my desires to those of any man, as Charlotte was able to do—even to one as understanding as Ed Rogers, my attorney and would-be fiancé for nearly two years now.

Whenever this feminine ambivalence frustrated me, I would think, Maybe later I'll change enough to be able to settle down with Ed and have a couple of kids, which I know he expects me to do if he waits long enough. But in my heart I doubt it will ever happen because I have too much respect—yes, and too much of my own kind of love—for Ed to deceive him. I am willing to share sex with him, and we have a mutually gratifying relationship. I am willing to listen to his frustrations and problems, to soothe or advise him, whichever seems appropriate. But I am not willing to give up my lucrative and often dangerous enterprises, and until I am, it is impossible to commit myself to one place, one house, one family. I know that he will give me up sooner or later, as two previous lovers did; yet somehow I hope the day of that decision won't come until I am fifteen or twenty years older, at an age when, as with Hamlet's mother, the heyday in my blood is tame and humble.

Charlotte very carefully strained the flowers from the tea, pouring it from the pot through a strainer into our cups. After she sat down, I remarked on how effective the decor of the kitchen was, and she explained that she had copied the yellow wall and garden-green frieze combination from a display in *Better Homes and Gardens*. Listening to us, you would have concluded that we were new neighbors at a Welcome Wagon get-acquainted meeting. Finally, convinced that Charlotte was not prepared to do it, I broached the reason for my being there.

"Dr. Mansfield suggested that I might help you solve a personal problem. Do you want to discuss it with me?"

"Yes. Yes, of course," Charlotte said, but then fell silent.

I waited ten or fifteen seconds.

"If you've changed your mind, it's perfectly all right."

"No, oh, no. It's just—well, I don't really know how to begin."

"When did you first realize that there was a problem? Begin there."

"I'm not sure when I first noticed. Em and I, ever since we first met almost, have been so together, almost like one person, you know? I could always feel his moods changing, and I pretty well knew what was changing them. He's a terribly hard worker and totally devoted to his business and to me and the kids."

Charlotte stopped to sip the sweet camomile, and I forced myself to sip as well. I wondered whether a touch of brandy would kill the medicinal flavor.

"We've always been absolutely frank with each other. From the very beginning it's been like that, because we need each other. More than other husbands and wives, I think. Through thirteen years we've never really quarreled. Em's been the perfect father when he's home, too. The children trust him just as they trust me. And now, all that's changed. Please! Help me find out what's happened!"

As she made this plea, tears coursed down her cheeks, though her voice was calm, in no sense hysterical.

"You've asked him what's bothering him, of course?"

"Not when I first noticed. I thought perhaps he was coming down with a cold or the flu, and didn't want to worry me with it. But later I asked. I had to. I couldn't stand his silence, his withdrawal from the family. I may have raised my voice, scolded even—I don't remember. It was very unpleasant."

"And?"

"He was shocked. He just stared at me, as if I were a strange woman he had never seen before. Then he kind of grunted, and went off someplace."

"That's the only time you've approached him about his changing behavior?"

"No. One night about a week ago, when we were in bed, I—I reached out in the dark and touched him. Intimately, you know? At first he responded, and I thought we would make love and maybe he would be all right again. But then he turned away, mumbled that he was tired, and that was the end of it."

"Do you suppose he may be suffering from some male disorder? A male menopause kind of thing, perhaps?"

"I don't think so. Neither does Liz."

"Something worse then. AIDS? Some physical thing?"

"Oh, no!"

"But a doctor hasn't examined him so far as you know?"

"I don't think so. But Em's a very practical person. If he was sick I'm sure he would go to a doctor."

"Sometimes people get ill mentally but don't realize what has happened to them."

"Yes, I know, but I don't think it's psychological. I don't know how I know but I do. Believe me!"

"I see. Then you think it's something that has happened to him. Blackmail, maybe."

"Something like that, yes."

"Have you access to his banking accounts?"

"Our joint accounts, yes. We share a money-market savings account and we have two CD accounts for ten thousand each. No money's been taken from those."

"But you know nothing about his business accounts?"

"No."

I sipped at my tea, which was now lukewarm and tasted worse than when it was hot. This didn't seem to be my kind of case any more than camomile was my kind of tea. Charlotte's problem, despite her own opinion and Big Sister's, seemed to me to be another woman. What she needed was a twenty-four-hour detective service that would never let sweet ole Em out of her sight. She had already rejected this possibility, of course, and to suggest it would only distress her, so I decided to play this interview to its routine conclusion, then telephone Dr. Mansfield with my decision not to undertake the case and my recommendation that she employ a surveillance agency to check on her brother-in-law's comings and goings.

"And you have found nothing among your husband's personal belongings that might suggest the source of the problem?"

"I wouldn't know what to look for."

"Does he have a work desk here, for example, a place where he keeps accounts or notes?"

"No. I pay all the household bills. The only desk is my secretary, and he never uses that."

"What about his clothes? Have you gone through the pockets of his suits and coats?"

"Only when I send them out for cleaning."

"Does he wear a different suit every day?"

"I think so. He has a dozen suits at least."

"When did you last send some out for cleaning?"

"I don't know. Three weeks ago, I guess."

"Well, you know, Charlotte, you can't intuit solutions to human problems. You have to have something to go on before you can begin an investigation. Would you mind if we went through the pockets of your husband's clothes to see whether we can find some clue to his problem? And yours."

"Now?"

"Right now, yes."

"Well, I don't know. It doesn't seem right. I mean . . ."

"Charlotte, I can't help you if you won't help me."

For a moment I thought she would refuse and I knew what was going through her mind. Such an overt deed sprung from suspicion would constitute an irrevocable violation of her until-now pristine trust in the great Emmett Harvey. She was like a patient with a pain that might be a symptom of cancer. If she ignored it, endured it, perhaps nature might heal it and all would be as lovely as before. But if she went to the doctor for a diagnosis, it might indeed turn out to be cancer and life, what was left of it, would be unending mortification and suffering. I let her struggle to a decision, which she reached with a deep sigh.

"I suppose that it would be all right," she said, rising to lead me to the master bedroom.

It must have been the largest room in the house, because despite its complete bath, a king-sized bed, chaise longue, two dressers with mirrors, and two walk-in closets—his and hers—it was uncluttered and airy. The two closets presented a study in contrast: Charlotte's was a potpourri of suits, prints, sport attire, luggage, shoes, hatboxes, sweaters, skeins of wool, knitting magazines, paperbound books, two pairs of skis tilting precariously from corners; Emmett's was as orderly as a pharmaceutical storeroom. He had a scheme for storage. His shoes were on racks and progressed from black through the color range to white. His suits were similarly arranged, beginning with a black tuxedo at the least accessible end of the rod, and moving through black pinstripe to plain navy blue, blue striped to gray, and gray pinstripe to brown and variations of brown, to one mild green and one subdued maroon. Then came the summer suits, and finally the sport jackets and their coordinated trousers. The shirts were laid flat on shelves opposite the suits, the whites together, the stripes together, then the solid colors. Emmett was an orderly man, with a place for everything and everything in its place, who would have made a first-rate submarine sailor. It was easy to understand why Charlotte would hesitate to disturb this filing cabinet of a closet, why she preferred to stand just inside the door as I conducted my search. I skipped the tuxedo and worked through the pockets of the jackets and suit coats, discovering in total seventy-five cents in change, two Bic pens, and three paper matchbooks all from the same businessmen's lunch lounge, the Colorado Beef House.

I had detected nowhere in the house the odor of cigarettes, cigars, or pipe tobacco, so I asked Charlotte whether Emmett smoked.

"No. Neither of us does."

"Do you two often go to this Colorado Beef House?"

"I've never been there," she answered, then added, "It must be a place where Em goes for lunch. Probably with clients."

"Does he drink much alcohol?"

"Oh, no. Sometimes when we go out to dinner we'll have a glass of white wine with our meal, and we always have a bottle of Mumm's on New Year's Eve—it's sort of a tradition with us, but we don't as a rule drink at all. Emmett says it doesn't give him a good image in his business, and it's a waste of money."

I gave her the change and the two pens, but I pocketed the matchbooks because I had noticed something about all three: on the blank inside cover of each was pencilled a number: "at 4" read one, "at 5" another, then just "4."

"Emmett sounds like a man with no bad habits," I commented as we returned downstairs.

"Well, almost none," she said.

"Oh?"

"Once in a while, he likes to gamble."

"Gamble?"

"Play poker. But he says it isn't really a gamble because he usually wins. He's very good at it."

"Where does he play?"

"Until about a year ago, once a month with a group of brokers. But he quit that because it was too easy. Then for a while he used to fly to Las Vegas or Atlantic City on weekends every six weeks or so."

"You never went with him?"

"No. I didn't want to leave the children overnight with a sitter. And the dog. He would have to have been put up in a kennel."

"When did he last fly off?"

"It's been a while. Not since this change came over him. Maybe three months ago."

Charlotte offered me more tea but I declined "with alacrity," as a Victorian novelist might have written. At the door she asked whether I would be able to help her.

"I truly don't know," I answered. "Let me think about it and ask a few questions here and there. I'll call your sister when I've decided, but I don't want to mislead you. If your husband's problem is emotional, there's absolutely nothing I could do to help."

3

"Businessmen's lunch" usually means a good supply of steaks, sandwiches, fish of the day, and young waitresses in unbusinesslike scanties with such unparentally given names as Conchita, Lolita, Monica, JoJo. The Colorado Beef House and Lounge turned out to be one of the most popular such places in the northwest section of metropolitan Detroit. Its parking lot was crammed with Lincolns, Cadillacs, New Yorkers, Rivieras, and Tornados.

"Don't you feel just a bit cheap driving this little old Ciera?" I asked Ed Rogers as we swung into a parking slot between an Eldorado and a Mark VII.

"Not on your life," he said. "I own this baby, but I'll bet most of the cars in this lot are financed, leased, or company-owned."

I had asked Ed to escort me to the Colorado because I had enough common sense to realize that a businessmen's lunch place is not to be interpreted as a businessperson's lunch place despite the successes of women's lib. The waitresses at the Colorado, who wore what can charitably be described as short black midriff corsets, black panties, and black net stockings supported by garter belts, certainly did not look like liberated women. What they became after they left the job each day with more than one hundred dollars in tips, I don't know, though I rather suspect that their husbands or boyfriends did not find them so totally amenable as their customers did.

Nanette, the hostess, a perky-eyed brunette with the lean figure of a professional model and a pleasantly pitched tone of voice, escorted us to what I took to be a discreet corner table, where a lady with a gentleman friend would be out of the main line of viewing or being viewed. The location was fine for me, because I could stare wherever I could see without appearing to be rude or unduly curious.

"I can get us another table if you like," Ed said. "This is the boondocks."

"I couldn't be more content," I replied, reaching across the table and squeezing his hand as our waitress approached.

"I'm Nina. Can I get you something from the bar?" she asked, blinking prettily at Ed and ignoring me. She then bent over the table, presumably to write our order on her pad, and quite inadvertently revealed all but the nipples of her bulging breasts.

I ordered my usual up-Margarita (no ice), and Ed a lemon-twist martini on the rocks. After we were served by Nina—with a second mammarian exhibition—Ed asked the question I knew he would ask me sooner or later.

"Why are we here?"

"They're supposed to have excellent fish," I answered.

"So you said on the phone. But it won't be better than Moffat's, and with all these extras it's got to be a lot more expensive."

He opened the foot-and-a-half-long menu Nina had left.

"Ten ninety-five for whitefish," he said. "Andy sells it for half that price."

"Well, I'll pay for what I eat," I teased, "if you can't afford to."

His unblinking blue-eyed stare was the only answer I got, and though it was all a game, I knew it was over. Ed's a very tolerant man, but he sets limits, and I knew that I had stretched the tease line to the breaking point.

"All right," I said. "As if you didn't know. It's a possible new client."

"The owner of this joint's been taken by some hustler and has hired you as his bloodhound?"

"It's not the owner of this joint and you know very well that I can't tell you who the client is. Not unless I need legal advice, which will make him your client, too."

My relationship with Ed is sometimes as delicate as a gossamer thread, and it's a wonder that it's not been severed long before now. Being a modern man, he persists in pretending that he believes in equal rights for women; but being the man he is, half-English, three-eighths Norwegian, and one-eighth American Indian, he knows that men are stronger than women, as the lion is stronger than the lioness, and his heart believes what his mind denies: that fundamentally, women were created to serve men. The Greeks believed this, as did the Romans, the conquering Spanish, the empire-building English (Queen Elizabeth excepted), the Japanese and Chinese believe it to this day, as well as the Eskimos, the Russians, the Arabs, and no doubt the Fiji Islanders. Who is Ed Rogers to contradict such abundant witnesses?

"I'm still considering the case. I've reason to think this place might give me some clue as to whether there's a case at all. Right now, it doesn't seem likely. But we're here, so let's eat and enjoy."

I had lake trout and Ed ordered the day's special, "Strip Steak and Hash-fries." Both were served with a head of lettuce salad, very fresh, an Idaho baked potato, and small hard-crusted, slightly garlicized rolls. A uniquely spiced tartar sauce truly enhanced the fish meat. We had Piesporter wine with the meal.

"Well!" I said haughtily when we were finished and sipping coffee.

"Okay. So they serve good fish and decent steak. And even if you don't get a case out of it, we'll come back another time if you want to."

"And if I do?"

He had no opportunity to reply, for a tall man dressed in a semiformal black suit and carrying a case half the size of a briefcase stepped alongside our table, bowed from the waist like a Japanese maitre d', so that his Colonel Sanders goatee and flowing black cravat hovered over the tablecloth for a moment. He straightened up with a military snap and smiled, revealing a set of teeth the color of yellowed ivory.

"I trust that you enjoyed your lunch," he said.

"It was good," Ed replied.

"May I join you for a moment?"

Ed hesitated.

"Please do," I said.

Our guest pulled an empty chair from an adjoining table and sat down, partially blocking the aisle. He placed his case on the table in front of him.

"You the owner?" Ed inquired.

"Oh, no."

"Manager then?"

"No, no. Actually, I have nothing to do with the restaurant, although I have known the manager, Terry, all his life long. My name is Nathan."

He paused as if he expected us to recognize the name. Ed and I looked at each other, then at him.

"I deal in gold. Permit me to show you a few trifles."

Majestically, as if he were about to produce the eighth wonder of the world, he placed one lean hand atop his case, pressed the snap release, and opened the case to reveal, set in plush royal purple velvet, an array of bracelets, rings, and neck chains. In the dim restaurant light they gleamed soft and true. I am no jeweler, but

I have studied gems and jewelry because much of my business involves recovering stolen valuables, and I sensed that these were not fake.

One of Ed's more disagreeable characteristics is a tendency to erupt from time to time with righteous indignation.

"You mean to say that you slip around here interrupting people's lunches to peddle your junk, and the manager doesn't throw you out on your ass!"

"The manager, sir, recognizes fine jewelry. But if I offend you—"

Nathan quickly closed his case.

"No, no," I said. "My friend, Mr. Nathan, is—"

"Just Nathan, miss. My given name."

"My friend is sometimes mistaken in his evaluation of quality," I finished, and the look I concentrated on Ed got through to him. "Now I know a little about gold, and I really would like to look at your samples."

Slowly, Nathan again opened his case, this time turning it in my direction so that the upright lid hid the contents from Ed's eyes. While I looked at the display, Nathan spoke—more to Ed than to me.

"Not samples, miss. Artifacts—each individually wrought by an artist. A strange way to do legitimate business, you are thinking, yes? But easily explained. Gold has been my life's work, but age is now my master. I cannot take care of a shop as I once did. Every afternoon I must sleep for two hours—my heart requires it. I cannot earn too much money or I shall lose my Social Security. You will find all such things out in your time. But I know the several—there are only a half dozen at most—true goldsmiths in the area who still do each piece as a work of art. If they give their work to the galleries to sell, the gallery owner takes fifty percent of the price. Ah, but if I sell for them, I charge ten, sometimes fifteen percent. Everybody profits in his own way, for my price is much cheaper than a gallery's would be. I have no overhead, you see."

I was holding a gold chain necklace in my hand that must have weighed two ounces.

"And," Nathan continued, turning to me, "I come to meet many very nice people."

"And some not so nice, probably," I said, glancing at Ed. "This necklace, now. What does it weigh?"

Nathan consulted the back of a card which he drew from a pocket in the lid of the case.

"Weight: 983 grains. That would be about two and a quarter ounces. The work was done by Dante Lanzetti, whose name you may know."

"I'm afraid not."

"He teaches gold- and silversmithing at Michigan State University. In the evenings, he uses the university facilities to do his own work. Notice the linkage: delicate but very strong."

I had noticed the linkage as well as the gradation in size of each disc, like a pearl necklace with the largest pearls at the bosom cleft.

"It must be very expensive."

"It is the most expensive piece I carry, and I carry it now only because Christmas is near and I hope the spirit may move some generous gentleman to purchase it for his favorite lady."

"How much is expensive?" Ed asked.

Nathan again consulted his card.

"Forty-eight hundred and seventy-five dollars. In a gallery it would be marked to six thousand."

"In galleries people dicker," Ed said.

"Just so. But it should certainly bring more than five thousand after conversations."

"If you really want to sell that chain," Ed said, "you'd do better to hang around pro basketball locker rooms than restaurants."

I was now holding a pair of earrings of stretched gold strands, attached to a gold plate by gold knobs twice the size of the holes through which their strands depended. They looked like miniature wind chimes, and in the dimness of the restaurant they reflected light as dew reflects the sun.

"I love these," I said, and meant it.

Another card emerged from the lid pocket.

"They were done by Philip Pike," Nathan said.

"Him I've heard of," I said. "He won some award at a Chicago jewelry exhibition last winter, didn't he?"

"Exactly. His scarab variations won first award."

"How do we know he made these?" Ed asked.

"May I?" Nathan asked me, taking one of the earrings from my hand.

He produced a small tube flashlight from a vest pocket, and directed its beam on the back of the plate where, faintly inscribed, were the letters P-I-K-E.

"And how much are these?" I asked.

"Five hundred and twenty-five dollars, miss," Nathan recited from the appropriate card.

"Let me get this straight," Ed interrupted. "Do you expect us to believe that some people are gullible enough to take your word for the value and hand over to you hundreds of dollars for these trinkets?"

"Those who know me do. Those who do not, like yourselves, wish verification, of course. It is only natural and prudent. But I also must be prudent. What I suggest to a new customer, truly interested in a piece, is the following: leave me your name, address, identification—the number of your driver's license along with, perhaps, a confirmation of identity by means of a credit card, then take the item with you, have it appraised by any expert you choose, and return to discuss it with me another day. I can think of no fairer way of verification than that. There is one exception, of course: the Lanzetti necklace. The insurance I carry on it forbids such procedure.''

"Don't you lose a good many pieces letting people walk off with them like that?'' I asked.

Nathan smiled, and his yellowed teeth looked like diluted gold in the dim corner light.

"I have been pursuing my trade this way now for seven years. In that time only one item has been stolen on trust, so to speak. Of course, one needs an instinct about people. If I have the slightest doubt, I never trust.''

"Well, would you trust me to take these earrings for a day or two?''

"Possibly. Do you wish to take them?''

"Jane,'' Ed said, "as your lawyer, let me advise you not to involve yourself. He'll want a receipt, and when you return them . . .''

"No receipt is necessary,'' Nathan said to Ed, then to me, "although your attorney's advice is sound. There are scoundrels who misrepresent their jewelry, then claim that the item returned is not the item loaned. I assure you both, I am an honest merchant as your own jeweler's assessment will convince you. But please, feel no compulsion to take these if you do not truly think they will enhance your wardrobe.''

I already had my purse open. I drew out my wallet and laid my driver's license, my Visa card, and a Mobil credit card on the table in front of Nathan. He took a small gold pen from his coat pocket, and began copying onto a blank index card.

Ed sat fidgeting, occasionally shaking his head, presumably to indicate disapproval of my foolish behavior, but he was too well acquainted with me to voice a syllable of objection.

"You won't mind, I'm sure, if I request your telephone number?'' Nathan said.

I gave it to him.

"This is Tuesday," he said, packing his case up tidily after slipping the earrings into a two-by-three-inch envelope and handing it to me. "I shall be here again on Friday about the same time. Can I expect to see you then?"

"I'll be here," I said. "Thank you for your time. I hope it won't be wasted on me."

Standing now, Nathan bowed slightly, produced his dim gold smile, and walked off to the bar, where he stood for a time chatting with what I took to be some of the regular patrons.

"I suppose this means you've decided to take the new case?" Ed remarked.

"Not necessarily."

"You don't really trust that old huckster, do you?"

"I think I do. That's real gold he's selling, darling. I'd stake my virtue on it."

"If he's what he says he is, why's he done up in that ringmaster's outfit? And why does he talk like a queen of England ambassador?"

"Because, Mr. Rogers," I said, affecting a cockney accent, "with a laidy like meeself, 'ee wants ter show proper good manners, 'ee does."

When we left ten minutes later, Nathan had already gone. Ed had been right: I had decided to take on the case if only to discover whether there was a case to take on. What had brought me to this conclusion I cannot explain—the workings of the mind are abstruse and self-deceptive—but the style of the Colorado Beef House seemed so inconsistent with the character of Emmett Harvey as portrayed by his wife and Dr. Mansfield that I determined to find out whether the sisters were simply gullible dupes, or whether Emmett himself had been duped into a behavior pattern alien to his true character. Nathan might provide a starting point for me if I could get him off the subject of gold.

I wasted no time getting started. First, I called Bernie Woodward at the *Birmingham Eccentric,* and was lucky to catch him in before he left to relax with what he called his "juniper tranquilizers" after a hard day at the office. The office is the newsroom of the newspaper where he is a senior editor. Bernie and I have a mutual-aid arrangement: he researches newspaper files for me when I need information. I provide him with news items, which in my line of work are sometimes scandalously newsworthy.

"What do you know about a place called the Colorado Beef House?" I asked.

"Great place for scenery. Canyons and clefts galore. Food's not bad either."

"I want to know who owns it."

"Ever think of looking at the license to sell? It's got to be on public display."

"You know what I mean. I want to know what kind of person the owner is, whether he actually runs the operation, or is, maybe, a front for someone else. Whatever you can find out."

"You want to pay my expenses while I research the problem in the field?"

"I'll do that, Bernie, really I will."

"You must be desperate, J. D. But I owe you one. I'll get back to you maybe tonight. Tomorrow for sure."

Then I called Art Spring. Art's father had established Spring's Jewelry Store on Woodward just below Maple in 1916. After his father's retirement in 1957, Art had taken over the store and had run it profitably until three years ago, when two "junk" jewelers moved into town during what old-time Birmingham residents have come to call, with distaste, "The Great Expansion." In the past five years seven six-story high-rise office buildings have punctured the town's flat horizon like glaciers gliding south on a sea, and these have been quickly attended by their natural satellites—parking structures, insurance offices, quick- if not fast-food restaurants. "You can't compete honestly with silver and gold traders," Art kept complaining, and one year ago, after fifty-eight years in business, he sold his store and good will to Shifton's Jewelers. "At least," he explained, "they're first-class second-raters." He took a month's vacation in the Virgin Islands, then returned and advertised himself in the *Eccentric* as "available for gold and silver appraisals." I have worked for several of his more wealthy clients, and more than once he has appraised recovered jewelry for me.

"I want to show you some gold earrings," I told him. "I'll buy you a Rob Roy if you're going to Moffat's this afternoon."

"Three."

"Split the difference?"

"Deal."

When I got to Moffat's a little before five, Art was holding court in one of the several booths that faced the bar. An elderly lady with a slight blue tint in her gray hair was inhaling his opinions, staring into his pudgy face, which always reminds me of a redskin potato, as if she dared not miss the blink of a single wink. Alongside the booth, waiting his turn, was a tweed-clad stone-faced gentleman, as lean for his build as Art was stout for his. I wriggled into a seat at the bar between Bert McCafferty, Birmingham's most prosperous travel agent, and Susan Bronfelter, sales rep for a restaurant-supply company, whose giggling laughter after three glasses of wine ascends ubiquitously to the ceiling, as rising bubbles permeate a glass of freshly poured champagne. Susan had not yet reached the giggling stage, so I ordered a Margarita and we chatted inconsequentially for fifteen minutes until Pat, Art's waitress, tapped me on the shoulder.

"Mr. Spring would like to talk to you," she said.

31

I noticed as I sat down that his glass was empty, and told Pat to bring him a drink on me.

"How's Lillian?" I asked, trying not to notice his extruding English frog eyes blinking slowly, like Corvette headlights opening and closing.

"Bitchy as usual," Art replied. "She's been like that ever since I sold the store. Got nothing to do."

"There are lots of salesperson-wanted signs around town."

"No fun if she can't give the orders."

He shook his head sadly, as if I had just informed him of the death of a dear mutual friend. But then he brightened, and held his cupped left palm toward me.

"Lay it on me, baby. Time's a-wastin'."

I took Nathan's envelope from my purse and carefully slipped the earrings into Art's left hand. The index and middle fingers of his right hand plucked one earring up and dangled it a foot in front of his myopic eyes.

"Pike," he said. "Right?"

"You tell me."

He fished his jeweler's glass from a side pocket, inserted it into his eye socket, and examined the earring for a moment.

"Yeah, it's Pike. I'd know his work anywhere even without his signature. Stolen?"

"I don't think so, but they could be. Can you find out for me?"

"They're not on last month's police list. I'd remember if they were."

"Good."

"So what do you want to know?"

"How much are they worth?"

"Oh—hard to be exact. But it's good work. Pike doesn't do bad work, or doesn't sell it if he does. Delicate. Not easy to draw strands as consistently thin as these. Hmm. In a store, I'd guess somewhere between seven-fifty and nine hundred, depending on the overhead and the clientele. Okay?"

"Okay."

We sipped at our drinks. I became aware of a fidgety matron standing alongside the bar well but not drinking, making ill-concealed covert signals at Art.

"One more question. Ever hear of an elderly, very proper gentleman with a goatee named Nathan who sells jewelry in bars and restaurants?"

"Never did and don't want to."

"Thanks. One of your fans wants your autograph, I think."

I slid from the booth, caught Pat on her way to the barwell, and pointed toward Art's glass.

"Send my bill upstairs with Susan, please," I told her, laying a dollar on her tray.

4

"You sure this isn't some kind of gag? A birthday gimmick for me maybe, set up by Milly?" Harry asked.

"Harry, I don't have any idea when your birthday is, and I haven't talked to Milly since that bash you two threw last August. This is business pure and simple."

We were sitting in the office of my home apartment on the third floor of the Birmingham Tower. Earlier that morning I had phoned Dr. Mansfield and told her that I would like to investigate Charlotte's problem for a week or ten days, as I had a suspicion that might lead to something (or might not), but that I would need money to hire a private detective at eighty dollars a day plus expenses, and that I would want the apprentice job she thought she could get me in her brother-in-law's brokerage business. She didn't quibble. Half an hour later she called me back to say I had an appointment with Emmett at two-thirty.

It was now eleven-fifty. Harry Jenkins, whom I hire whenever I need routine surveillance, had nothing urgent on his schedule, and he responded promptly to my summons. But he couldn't believe the assignment.

"And all I have to do is lounge around at the Colorado Beef House for four or five hours a day, drinking and admiring the scenery?"

"That you'll do without my telling you to. But you'll also act as if you have some resources, because you're a pretty smart operator."

"Any particular kind of operator?"

"Use your imagination. But it better be something you know about."

"What am I looking for?"

"Anything off-color that might be interesting. But I'll give you a photo of the man I'm investigating this afternoon. He generally gets to the Colorado around four or five when he goes, which I don't think is too often. Keep an eye out for him."

"You want me to kind of become a regular there then?"

"A temporary regular, Harry—yes. Get to know some of the other regulars. See whether you can cuddle up to the manager or better still, the owner."

"How about the girls?"

"Them, too—up to a point. But remember Milly."

" 'Course, being a man of means, I can't drink lower-shelf booze."

"I should say not!"

"Glenlivet all the way."

I walked into the fifteenth-floor offices of Whitaker & Harvey five minutes before my scheduled two-thirty appointment, and presented myself to the middle-aged woman at the front desk, who appeared to serve as receptionist, typist, and general secretary to the staff of four men and one woman working as brokers.

"Mr. Harvey will be a little late, Miss Mulroy," she informed me. "Do sit down. There are magazines on the table there and lots of company reports."

I picked up a brochure on a mutual municipal bond fund and pretended to study its graphs, pictograms, and hypothetical statistics, while I was actually studying the personnel of Whitaker (from whom Harvey had purchased the company) & Harvey. They seemed suited to their jobs. A Mr. Perkins sat at the lead desk and appeared to be the most experienced as well as the oldest employee, since twice younger members came to consult him about phone calls. Perkins was about fifty-five, I guessed, bordering on stout. The other three men were much younger and wore jackets, rather than a conservative suit like Perkins, though all were generally conservative, especially in the selection of their ties. The one woman, whose nameplate I could not see but who, I discovered later, was Mrs. Melissa Duncan, also wore a wool suit with a blouse buttoned at the neck and a kind of bow tie. It was an efficient office with a competent staff, so far as I could see, with each person quietly pursuing his clients' interests by telephone and computer.

On the way here, I had stopped at the Harveys' Vanessa Street home to pick up a photo of Emmett for Harry, which I dropped off at his house; it was a true likeness, for I recognized Emmett the moment he opened the door to the office. He would have enhanced any billboard that hoped to portray the healthy American male doing what healthy American males do on billboards—smoke cigarettes, stir vodka, smile at healthy American females. He had an arrow-straight nose, firm chin with dimples alongside his mouth, square jaw, and the suggestion of a natural wave in his full head of chestnut brown hair. His body would have been a fit match for his handsome countenance if the stomach had been flat instead of ovoid: too little systematic exercise and too many calories had already shaped Emmett's midriff in the mold of the American business executive.

He paused at the receptionist's desk, spoke briefly to her, turned, and glanced at me, then went into the partitioned enclosure that was his private office. Two minutes later, the receptionist, named Essie Lucas, I was to find out later, said Mr. Harvey would see me now.

He rose politely from behind a desk too large for the small room, stepped forward to take my hand, and

gestured me to the chair alongside his desk, then resumed his seat.

"Dr. Mansfield called to ask whether I can be of
help to you," he said, all business immediately and
completely oblivious to my physical charms, which most
men take time to notice (and, more often than not, by
the silent communication of their roving eyes, to let
me know that they have noticed). "I'm not clear about
what you would like me to do, but I must tell you that
we are not in a position to hire any more help at this
time, Miss Malloy."

"It's Mulroy," I said. "Jane Mulroy, Mr. Harvey.
It's kind of you to see me even if you can't help me.
It's quite simple, really. A dear aunt of mine is a good
friend of Dr. Mansfield, and that's how I happen to
be here. I've had some unhappy experiences—a bad
marriage and a worse divorce—I won't bore you with
the details. After it was all over a couple of months
ago, I was at loose ends. My aunt, who has kind of
adopted me emotionally since her husband died some
years ago, thought I was about to have a nervous
breakdown, and, well, I don't know, maybe she was
right. She decided that what I needed was a career. I
have a University of Michigan bachelor of arts degree,
and I can type accurately and fairly fast, so she con-
tacted some of her friends' husbands with the idea of
placing me in offices of different kinds, hoping that I
would find something I might study seriously. So far
I've worked in a bank and in a real-estate office. I
can't say that either filled me with enthusiasm.

"If you think I'd be a nuisance here for a week or
so, just say so. I think I'm doing these things as much
to please Aunt Emily as to keep myself busy. Of course,
I shouldn't expect any pay."

Now for the first time Emmett Harvey really looked
at me—as an individual rather than as an item in his
immediate environment. He wasn't used to people vol-

unteering to do anything useful for absolutely nothing.

"So you're trying to find a career that you might like, is that it?" he asked.

"That's what I'm hoping for."

"You realize, don't you, that this business is mainly selling. Like real estate."

"Oh yes. But in real estate you have to locate people who want or need a new house. I should think stocks and bonds would be different. If people with money don't know what to do with it, your job would be to sell them the idea of investing it someplace other than a bank."

"That's true, Miss—or is it Mrs.?"

"Mizz will do nicely."

"Well, that's true, Miss Mulroy, but you still have to find people who have money. Do you have a lot of friends with money they don't know what to do with?"

The sixty-four-thousand-dollar question! Did I have a lot of such friends? Harry? Harry had to finance the queen-size bed he just bought to ease Milly's aching back. Bernie Woodward? I remembered "Bachelor Bernie" telling me last year that he had considered setting up an IRA, but when he realized that he'd have to cut his "martini sustenance in half," he had abandoned this idea. Ahmad had a lot of money on paper but it was all invested in his karate club, and whenever he accumulated an excess, it went right back into improvements. Andy Moffat, of course, had a couple of million at least, but I was sure he had his own investment counselors and wouldn't appreciate advice from a newly ordained apprentice broker, however brilliant she might be. Some of my former satisfied clients might be willing to make a token purchase out of gratitude if I approached them, but I knew I wouldn't— couldn't—jeopardize my true profession by such menial tactics. There was, of course, Aunt Emily and her circle of wealthy society friends.

"Perhaps a few," I said with a smile. "But of course, I would have to know more about the kind of investments your company offers before I could consider actually approaching them."

"Indeed you would," Harvey said. "And you would have to secure your broker's license, too. Well, I see no harm in helping you, and I hope we can."

He clicked open the intercom to the receptionist's desk.

"Essie."

"Yes, Mr. Harvey?"

"Will you ask Mrs. Duncan to come in, please?"

When Mrs. Duncan appeared, wearing freshened lipstick and perhaps a refortifying dab of Chanel No. 5, Harvey rose, more to indicate that my interview was over, I think, than out of politeness to Mrs. Duncan.

"Melissa, this is Jane Mulroy. She'll be working with us for a short time in order to get some idea of how we operate. Would you be kind enough, please, to show her the ropes? Let her watch you operate for a couple of days?"

"Yes, of course, Mr. Harvey," Mrs. Duncan replied in a tone of cultivated sycophancy.

But her eyes as she surveyed me were as hostile as those of a tired old cobra cornered by a hungry mongoose.

We went to her desk, and I sat down in one of the chairs reserved for her clients.

"I'll be with you in a minute," she said, and busied herself stuffing copies of a company report into eight or nine envelopes that had already been addressed. She was over forty, but not over forty-five, I decided. If I were required to describe her in two words or less, I would choose "tidy" and/or "neat." Lots of people are tidy but not neat, and vice versa, but Melissa Duncan was both—about her person and her belongings. Not only were her shoelaces tied, they were tied in symmetrical knots with all string ends of equal length. I suspected that she not only measured the curls on each side of her head but also counted them to make certain that each side had the same number. She had rinsed her hair a light brown with a hint of copper, and I'm sure that she had touched up her eyebrows with the same mixture. Her eyes were nearer green than brown, her figure, unsurprisingly, was as trim as an Olympic gymnast's, and her posture, both sitting and standing, was unrelentingly erect. Her desk reflected her personality. I was sure that anyone who knew her could walk into an empty office usually occupied by fifty people with fifty desks and select the one that belonged to Mrs. Duncan.

"Now," she said at length, after rubber-banding her package of stuffed and sealed envelopes, "exactly what is it you wish to know, Miss Mulroy?"

Did I detect a note of suspicion in her tone?

Never infer meaning from tone of voice, only facts count! I reminded myself of Rule 19 (or 29 or 39) from my yet-to-be-written manual for private investigators.

"Please call me Jane," I said, with what I think of professionally as my *weltschmerz* smile.

In my business a woman needs many faces to project the image she hopes to transmit to her viewers. There is the *joie-de-vivre* countenance when one wishes to present oneself as the gay giddy gal of every man's fantasy lovelife, who asks for nothing more than the thrill of his presence over a martini, on a carousel, in bed—wherever he chooses to be. Then there is the furrowed-brow face of confusion, useful in various situations, but primarily whenever one needs time to react. And of course, I have my slow-Jane face, designed to reinforce the opinion (often held by people I deal with who don't know that they are dealing with me) that I am more dimwitted than most people and on the whole unobservant of details. But right now the *weltschmerz* smile seemed appropriate to convey the impression that the world was definitely not too much with me, nor I with it; that the cherries in my bowl of life had turned into prunes; that I was trying to tolerate life a little longer in the hope that I might miraculously discover some mundane routine with which to pass my days until I would be relieved forever of the burdens of mortality. It had an effect on Mrs. Duncan.

"Are you quite certain that you wish to learn the brokerage business, my dear?"

"No. I mean, well, I want to learn to do something from day to day. You see, I've recently been divorced and I've been under a great strain for a long time, but now it's all over and, you see, well, I just don't know what to do with myself."

"You wouldn't be doing it just for the money? I don't mean to inquire into your personal affairs, believe me, but—"

"Money?" I interrupted, as if the word were new to my vocabulary. "Goodness no! Money is the least of my worries. Time is my problem. Do you know what it's like to finish up what household chores you have— there aren't many in a small apartment—by nine o'clock in the morning, and then wonder what you're going to do for the next thirteen or fourteen hours? Oh, I know working women who think that would be the next thing to paradise, who think they would shop all day long, or go to the movies every afternoon, but believe me, one month of that routine is about all any woman in her right mind can stand. Why, sometimes it seems—"

I stopped in mid-sentence and clicked on my repentant grimace.

"I'm sorry! Taking up your time with my personal problems. Forgive me!"

"That's perfectly all right, Jane. If we're going to work together, we probably ought to know something about each other. Tell you what. I've one phone call I must make, and then I'll be done for the day. Do you drink at all?"

"I like a glass of wine now and then."

"Good. I'll make my call and then we'll go over to the Little Foxes for half an hour or so, and I can explain the basics of this business. Okay?"

The Little Foxes was a lunchroom bar-restaurant in a miniature mall sandwiched in between a reputable jeweler's and the district offices of a major life insurance carrier. A pseudo-oak bar ringed the center of the room, like the hole in a doughnut, and booths lined all the walls. The bar was for the clerks and lawyers and shoe salesmen and accountants whose daily routines demanded the periodic relaxation of "a quick one," whereas the booths were for the lunch crowd, composed in the main of half-hour eaters, and for after-hour lingerers metamorphosing from their business personality of Jekyll to their home image of Hyde, or vice versa. We arrived about forty-five minutes before the post-work rush, and the room was nearly deserted. I was not surprised to hear Mrs. Duncan order a perfect Manhattan. I settled for a glass of Liebfraümilch.

"I usually stop here after hours to unwind a bit," Mrs. Duncan confided, and added as a matter of fact, "though, being alone, I usually sit at the bar."

"Do the men also stop by for a drink after work?"

"On no. This place is too tame for our crowd. They go to Bimbo's, or the Nineties—you know, someplace where the waitresses wear short skirts and you can make a bet on a horserace or a football game."

"I see. Someplace like the Colorado Beef House."

"I don't know that place, but if there are girls there and gamblers, they'll know it."

"Isn't going to such places bad publicity for the company?"

"You would think so, and I guess thirty years ago it might have been. But everybody's into the market these days in one way or another—plumbers, preachers, and go-go dancers, too, and our reps claim they pick up quite a few accounts after hours at bars."

"Do you believe that?"

"Well, Tony D'Amato probably does. He's been divorced three times and is a real swinger, from what I hear."

"What about your boss?"

"Oh, no! He'll take a drink at a brokers' conference, of course, but he doesn't drink regularly. A fine man, Mr. Harvey. Devoted to his family. Comes in every morning at the stroke of nine, but he'll work till all hours whenever it's necessary."

"How often is that?"

"I don't really know, dear," Mrs. Duncan said, peering at me suspiciously. "Why do you ask?"

"I always assumed that a broker's office closes when the markets close."

She relaxed, sipped her Manhattan, and then with a smug smile said, "You do have a lot to learn about this business, Jane. But let's put it off till tomorrow, shall we, and have one more drink today."

So we put off my learning about the brokerage business, but we learned a lot about each other. Mrs. Duncan learned that my husband, whom I had thought to be a diligent and enterprising young junior executive, had deceived me from the beginning. He began wasting my inherited savings gambling and taking long "business" trips with nonbusiness associates of the opposite sex, and finally had tried to brutalize me physically when I confronted him with his offenses. Sometimes I think I should have been an actress. When I am lying, I have a talent for so totally empathizing with my mythical self that I can without effort evoke tears, and for reasons I cannot explain, tears convince ninety-nine out of a hundred people that one is telling the truth.

I learned that Mrs. Duncan's husband, with whom she lived for a little over one year twenty years ago, had been an insufferable slob. He left his dirty underwear and socks on the bedroom floor instead of putting them down the clothes chute or in the laundry basket; he never emptied the ashtrays he dirtied with his cigarette butts; he expected her to clean up the slop-dried stains of his daily shaving and tooth-cleaning routines; and he was totally undiscerning, being unable to distinguish a fine Martex fluff towel from the plain Kresge kitchen towel she expected him to use when he cleaned his hands after working on his silly little sports car. No matter how hard she tried to teach him, he could never knot his tie neatly, and he never polished his shoes or thought to have them polished. It was too much for her to bear through a lifetime, and they had been divorced "without prejudice on either side," Mrs. Duncan assured me in evidence of her humanity toward mankind.

When I asked her what kind of man Mr. Harvey was, I thought I was listening to a graveside eulogy. He was wholesome, he was neat, he was prompt, he was reliable, he loved his wife and children, he did not use profanity or vulgarisms, and so forth—it was apparent that Mrs. Duncan had developed a maternal affection for Mr. Harvey that, except for her orderly nature, she would have preferred to be Oedipal.

We parted without prejudice on either side and with a promise to get to work on me in the morning.

5

One of the advantages of working without pay is that one can pretty well set one's own hours. Brokers, like bank clerks, have work to do before their doors open and work to do after they close. Contrarily, a private investigator doesn't keep specified hours. She (or he) may work forty-eight hours without a break, then wait doing nothing for three days and nights. The waiting is often the most difficult part of the job, and whenever I can I try to avoid it. That's why the next morning at exactly five minutes past nine I picked up my phone and dialed Bernie Woodward at the *Eccentric*. Editors, I knew, keep very rigid hours no matter how severe their headaches (read "hangovers") may be.

But this morning Bernie sounded as fresh as a robin's welcome to the dawn of a bright spring day.

"Hey," he responded to my greeting. "Make a wish, J. D."

"Why?"

"I was actually reaching for the phone to call you when your call came in. You know, like when two people at the same moment say the same thing?"

"Uh-huh. I've made my wish. Now prove that it wasn't made in vain."

"Grumpy, aren't you. Okay. Lemme see here. Yeah. Colorado Beef House," he said, adopting his reading tone of voice, "License issued to Terence Garfinkel, November 15, 1984. I checked on him in our files and Alan Trimball checked him out for me in the *Free*

Press files. That's why I couldn't get back to you last night. Nothing on him, of course. There wouldn't be anything very negative or the Commission wouldn't have authorized his license."

"Well, thanks anyway."

"Hold on. Did you know the previous owner was ordered to get rid of the place?"

"Who and why?"

"Emmanuel d'Elessandro. That's a small d and a capital E. Why? Conviction for carrying enough coke in his car to be sold for profit. He claimed a customer, whose name he didn't know, had given it to him to take to a party to which he was invited to give to a friend of the unknown customer, who would identify himself at the party. Nobody bought the story."

"Where's he now?"

"He did five months in Jackson, got paroled, and he hasn't reported to me since."

It was too early to check with Harry, who had no reason to get out of bed before ten or eleven, especially when in the line of duty he was endangering his liver with too much Glenlivet, so I made myself a cup of coffee and sat drinking it, staring at the Financial News Network on cable. A bosomy redhead with an upsweep hairdo and an English accent was chattering away, listing yesterday's future option prices—the precious metals first, then the grains, oils, hog bellies—on and on. I wondered whether there was a futures quote on private investigators' chances of survival if they interfered with the future profits of big-time drug dealers with Mafia connections.

Half an hour later, I was carefully attaching Nathan's gold earrings, which in a few hours I expected to own. They were really too dressy for the office, but I decided to wear them anyway in order to get Melissa's reaction. It was not long in coming.

"They're fantastic earrings!" she commented while I was arranging a stack of new company reports in alphabetical order. "Where on earth did you buy them?"

"They're the work of a goldsmith named Pike," I said. "He's quite well known hereabouts."

"I shouldn't wonder," she replied, reaching out to touch the strands with the tips of her fingers. "Quite expensive, I should imagine."

"Yes," I said, and then was silent.

During the ensuing hour and a half I learned how to use some of the many manuals and record books so abundant in financial offices—Standard & Poor's monthly and weekly reports, Moody's business annuals on industrials, utilities, financial institutions, Value Line data—well, suffice it to say that Melissa Duncan, having taken a liking to me, was resolved to leave no gaps of ignorance in my basic training. Somehow she managed to get her own work done, as well as to supervise my education, and she was quite surprised, and perturbed, when at eleven-thirty I announced that I had to leave for lunch.

"It's an engagement I made before I knew I'd be here," I explained to mollify her somewhat, but Melissa was not easily mollified. She shrugged her shoulders, a gesture of impatience with her, almost said something, then pouted off to the privacy of her desk.

I arrived at the Colorado Beef House a few minutes before the major influx, and was flattered that Nanette remembered me at once.

"Would you like the same table you had before?" she inquired, and I assented gladly.

I didn't expect Nathan for at least half an hour and the vantage point of a rear table with a view suited me very well. Once again Nina was my waitress, and she wasted no time getting to me.

"Will you be eating alone?" she asked, preparing to remove the second place setting.

"I will, yes, but I'm expecting a friend in half an hour or so. You know him. Nathan?"

She stared hard at me for a moment, then smiled. "Those are his earrings, aren't they, honey?"

"They'll be mine if I buy them."

"They're beauts all right."

"Do you know Nathan well?"

"Just from talking with him in here. He comes round maybe twice a week. Never drinks nothing but decaf. Sweet old gent. He sold me a pin for ten dollars that everybody says is worth fifty in the stores."

"Does he live near here?"

"I don't know. Never thought to ask."

I took a long shot.

"Does Terry buy much from him?"

"Terry! Hah! Terry wouldn't buy cookies from a starving Girl Scout!"

"That tight, is he?"

Nina glanced about behind her, then bent low over the table so that for a moment the fragrant fumes of her Charlie obliterated the permeance of fry odors.

"You'd think he worked for IRS the way he gouges our tips for Social Security."

Then a thought occurred to her, and she straightened up almost militarily.

"You a friend of Terry's?"

"Oh no. But my brother is a friend of Mr. d'Elessandro."

"Who?"

"The man who used to own this place."

"Oh."

"Don't you know him?"

"Nuh-uh. He never comes in. Least not when I'm here. What'll you have to drink?"

It was not difficult to identify Terry as I sipped at my Piesporter wine and appeared to peer at the menu. A slight man, balding from the center of his head forward so that his dark hair formed a horseshoe halo above his pallid face, he bustled from kitchen to reservation desk to bar, and was greeted nowhere with a smile. The pencil-line mustache that he wore did nothing to enhance his appearance, nor did the designer gold-rimmed spectacles that were too large for his small face. Like many men small of stature as well as of character, he substituted a harsh officiousness for confidence and became an unpleasant caricature of the authority he endeavored to represent.

I ordered a salad and orange roughie, and had just finished eating when Nathan, dressed as impeccably as before, but wearing a dark blue suit now, bowed before me like a Japanese waiter, then placed his case on the tabletop opposite me and sat down. Without being summoned, Nina placed a cup of black coffee on the table for him.

"May I assume, Miss Mulroy, since you are wearing the earrings, that you have decided to purchase them?" Nathan asked with his gold-toothed smile.

"You may," I replied. "How do I make out the check?"

"You are quite satisfied as to their value then?"

"Quite."

"An old man like myself is more interested in the satisfaction of his customers than in making a profit. Thirty years ago—even ten– though I might have said some such thing—it would not have been entirely true. But now, with the grave moving closer each hour of the day, accumulating money seems the least important endeavor in man's life."

"Believe me, I'm entirely satisfied, Mr. Nathan."

"Just Nathan will do."

"Yes, you told me. But for me to address you by your first name seems somehow impertinent. I mean . . ."

What did I mean? He sat slightly smiling with his hands clasped in front of him, for all the world like a contented rabbi or Buddha.

"I mean, you're so dignified and formally correct, you know?"

"And old."

"I guess so, but you can't be much over seventy, and that's not old these days."

"Seventy-seven, Miss Mulroy."

We were having a polite conversation and he was obviously enjoying it, but I was accomplishing nothing for the doctor or Mrs. Harvey, so I tried to change the direction of our chitchat into a channel that might be more profitable to me.

"You stop in here every week, do you, Nathan?"

"Twice, sometimes three times a week."

"You must know everyone who stops in regularly then. I would think you'd have exhausted your market after a few months."

"An honest broker never exhausts his market. If in future you wanted to buy a gold necklace, Miss Mulroy, would you consult me, do you think, knowing how I operate?"

"Of course."

"So do others to whom I have sold. I'm not a peddler who harasses customers. I'm here if they wish to consult me. My presence reminds them of my availability, but I never approach them with a sales talk after the first sale."

"Does Terry buy much from you?"

"Terry isn't interested in gold. Or silver or diamonds. A very practical man is Terry, but a bit unimaginative, I'm afraid. However, as the French say, *chacun à son goût.*"

"You must know most of the regular customers, coming here as often as you do."

"Indeed I do."

"Most of them, well, the regulars I mean, are three-martini-lunch businessmen on credit accounts, I imagine."

"Quite a few, yes. Others come for the food."

"And to look at the pretty waitresses."

"Of course. It breaks the monotony of their working day. Do you object to their—uh—costumes?"

I stared at Nina's buttock cheeks for a moment as she delivered the tab to a table of three paunchy middle-aged men down the aisle.

"Not really. Everyone has to make a living with whatever talents God's given them."

"Very true. And if I may say so, Miss Mulroy, your own God-given beauty exceeds most of these waitresses'."

"You're an old flatterer, Nathan."

I feigned an embarrassed smile, then hurriedly changed the subject.

"Tell me, does Mr. d'Elessandro still own this place?"

"You know him?"

"No, but an acquaintance of mine does. Or used to. When I told him that I'd been here, he said Manny d'Elessandro owns the Colorado Beef House."

"I'm afraid he's not very close to Mr. d'Elessandro."

"Oh?"

"He sold out about a year ago."

"I'm not really surprised. My friend is a name-dropper who pretends to be on intimate terms with anyone of substance. Name a politician and he knows his sister or brother if not himself. You know the type?"

"Ah yes. A four-flusher. The term, as you probably know, comes from the game of poker."

"Really? How's that?"

"Well, in poker, a flush is five cards of the same suit. You understand?"

"I've never played poker, but I know that every player gets five cards, if the Western movies are right."

"They are. Now five cards of the same suit is usually a winning hand. But if you have only four and pretend that you have five?"

"Four-flusher?"

"Exactly! A pretender to a power that one does not possess."

Maybe, I thought, we're getting someplace now. Harvey loved the game of poker. Was there a connection between the Colorado Beef House and big-time poker games?

"Do you play much poker, Nathan?"

"One of the major pleasures in my life, Miss Mulroy, is playing poker on Saturday afternoons with a few friends who, like myself, have exceeded their three-score years and ten on this earth."

"Please call me Jane."

"Of course."

"It's nice that you and your friends can afford to gamble."

"Well, to be truthful, it's not really gambling, Miss— Jane. Gambling money, the old saying goes, has no home. It can't stay in one place very long. This week I win, next week I lose. When you play with the same people and the same stakes every week, it evens out. The companionship—camaraderie rather—that is what all of us win each week, you see?"

"Are your stakes very high?"

"Twenty-five and fifty."

He peered stern-faced across the table at me, then added, "cents," and chuckled.

"Well," I said, smiling, "my four-flusher friend seems to have been wrong again. He told me that this is a hangout for high-stake gamblers."

Nathan, still smiling, stroked his goatee with his right hand, as if he were milking a goat.

"No, he was right about that."

He leaned forward and lowered his voice.

"At the far end of the bar, the big man in the checked jacket, Mr. B. T. Hickory, has been known to bet twenty-five thousand dollars on a single horse race. The two friends with him, his bodyguards, people say, think nothing of betting a thousand dollars on a horse they favor."

B. T. Hickory was perched in his bar chair past the right angle turn of the bar, and occupied the center of the six-foot extension to the bartender's exit. His "friends" stood one on each side of him.

"He looks like a colorful character," I said. "Reminds me of Sydney Greenstreet."

"I see what you mean. And his two associates would have appealed to Damon Runyon. The little one with the heavy glasses and the scarred nose they call Tiny Tim. Rumor has it that he's deadly with a knife at twenty paces. I don't know about that, but I know for a fact that he always wears a small revolver strapped above his left hip, because I have seen it more than once. The big fellow with the cauliflower ears, twisted nose, and scar tissue about his eyebrows is Bulldog Janescu, who was a light-heavyweight contender of some stature ten or twelve years ago. He's always been a quiet gentleman when I've been here, but there are stories about his exploits in the late hours, when Hickory has had altercations with other customers."

"I'd think the manager, Terry, would bar them from the place."

"Not likely. They spend a great deal of money here, and on occasion rent the banquet hall in back for large parties. Even a mean dog is tolerant of the man who feeds it regularly."

"What does Mr. Hickory do to earn the money he gambles with and spends here?"

"People speculate about that. Real estate, some say, slum apartments. Stock-market profits, others think. I have no idea and prefer not to speculate about matters that don't concern me."

"Did you ever sell him any of your jewelry?"

"He is, in fact, my most steady customer. Every Christmas he buys half a dozen gifts from me. I'm hoping this year that he will purchase the Lanzetti necklace."

At this moment, wearing a maroon blazer and navy blue slacks, with a Racing Form tucked under one armpit, Harry Jenkins entered the Colorado, hesitated to adjust his eyes to the dim light, then swaggered to the bar and slouched into a seat near Hickory's end. Harry the horseplayer—it wasn't exactly what I had in mind when I told him to become a smart operator. But what had I expected—that he turn himself into a greenmail corporate raider? Or a Teamster official? Harry knew about horses, all right, as Milly will tell you on little or no provocation. I never had considered him a "smart" horseplayer, but then I wouldn't consider anyone who plays the horses regularly smart. And if what Nathan had said about Hickory and his pals was true, Harry might have made the right choice.

It was time that I thought about getting back to my own smart operation at Whitaker & Harvey, so I glanced at my watch, flicked on the oh-my-God-I'm-late face, and said to Nathan, "I'm running late. How shall I make out the check, Nathan?"

"I should be delighted to buy you another wine, Jane."

"I'd love one, but I'm starting out on a new job and I've got to get back to my training session."

"One of the advantages of aging, in addition to acquiring wisdom, is independence from the tyrant clock. Ah well. Make it out to Nathan, Inc."

I did as instructed and handed it to him.

"I hope you will return soon. I have enjoyed our conversation."

54

"Do you have a card so that I can call you if I should want something else? Christmas isn't far off."

"You can always find me here, Jane, on Tuesdays and Fridays at a bit past noon. It is my routine."

He was standing now, and gallantly moved behind me to pull out my chair as I stood up. When I walked past the bar on my way out, Harry was poring over the tables in the Racing Form, and Hickory seemed to be watching him.

6

Harry came to see me at a little past noon on Saturday. He had been on the job three days now and felt, since the Colorado didn't open on Saturday until four o'clock, that it was time to report. Which was fine except that, so far, he really had nothing to report.

"A lot of traffic goes through that place between eleven-thirty A.M. and two P.M., and a lot more between five and nine, you know? It's kinda like a barber shop. Each girl seems to have her own following, guys who want to sit at a table she's serving, and quite a few are even willing to wait at the bar until a place opens up for them. Weird."

"Different men have different tastes, Harry, for which womankind is grateful."

"I guess so. Your man hasn't shown while I've been there. He's sure no regular."

"I know that. I just want to know what he does and who he talks to on the occasions when he does go there. What do you know about the big goon who was sitting at the end of the bar when you came in yesterday?"

"That's B.T. He's a regular and he's sweet on the P.M. bartender, a big blond trick called Lorelei who weighs about half as much as Buford Hickory."

"Buford?"

"Sho' 'nuff, ma'am. Boo-ford T. Hickory from down Sowth Caw-line-nah way."

"You've heard of him before?"

56

"No, but one of his arms is Rick Janescu, who I've seen a couple times at Hazel Park Track. Nice guy, really, but a sucker for a tout."

"He's the one who was a prizefighter?"

"Right. And a damn good one too. I saw him get off the floor and kayo Pete Abrozzi on TV about ten, twelve years ago. I remember because I won a sawbuck on that fight from a guy standing next to me at Vito's Lounge in Hazel Park."

"Fascinating!"

"Sure, but useful. I told Rick about it first time I saw him at the Colorado, and I bought him a drink— you know, belated thank you. And he introduced me to Mr. Buford Hickory."

"What's Hickory's racket?"

"Rick didn't tell me that, and it didn't seem right to ask him right off. Want me to find out?"

"I want you to find out, yes, and whatever else you can about him, and the squirt with the gun who's always with him too. People call him Tiny Tim. As I understand it, Rick and Tim are Buford's bodyguards."

Harry stared at me with a mock expression of humiliation.

"You sure you need little ole me, J. D.? You work a lot faster than I do, seems like."

"What else do you know about the place?"

"Well, the manager is a drip called Terry. His main talent seems to be to make himself obnoxious to everyone who works for him, though he's sickeningly humble in the presence of patrons. He must be a good book man because he's a lousy personnel director."

"What about the cocktail crowd?"

"Mostly salesmen with expense accounts, and the owners or part-owners of the shops all over the northeast section. You know, tool-and-die shops, plastic manufacturers, auto parts. A dozen or so appear to come in every afternoon and pretend to put the make on the girls. A couple may be succeeding, I don't know, but most of the girls seem hardworking critters with husbands or children from divorced husbands. I doubt that many of them go the call-girl route, but what do I know about that? An innocent like me."

"Uh-huh. Anything else?"

"Not much. Cook's a guy named Chester. Chef Ches the girls call him, and he can be a terror on occasion, I gather from what they say to each other waiting at the well for drinks. I haven't seen him. Then there's Willie."

"Willie?"

"Yeah. He's the handyman. Lots of bars have guys like him around. To fix the washers in the restroom taps, bring buckets of ice to the bar, change light bulbs, be a spare busboy when things get real busy—you know. He's a little old man in the mid-sixties, hump-shouldered. Never needs to be told what to do, does it before he has to be told, I guess."

"Okay. Stick it out another week. By then I'll know whether I have a case or not."

"One other thing, J. D."

"What?"

"I could use an advance on expenses. That's a cash bar and I don't use a credit card, y'know?"

"I know, and I know why, too. Okay. How much?"

"Four hundred?"

"You can't be spending more than thirty dollars a day on my assignment, Harry. Two hundred should do."

And, so far as I shall ever know, it did. Harry said he would call me later in the week, but Wednesday came and went, as did Thursday. I was busy with Melissa, watching her when she was occupied and at the same time trying to follow Mr. Harvey's movements, and frustration was beginning to take its toll as each day passed and I discovered nothing that seemed the least bit relevant to my quest, which is a word I often use to dignify my endeavors when they're not justifying themselves. Harvey himself paid little attention to me, beyond asking me once or twice how I was doing when we came face to face in the performance of our tasks. I spent most of my time checking on the ratings of new bond issues and discouraging Tony d'Amato from getting close enough so that he could have an excuse for touching me—with his hands, hips, shoulders, knees. Tony was a toucher. He seemed to believe that contact with his flesh would discharge currents of desire in any woman, and in a way he was right—I don't recall encountering a man I desired more to floor with a jujitsu arm twist or a karate neck chop. A slight man barely two inches taller than I in his high-heeled shoes, he reeked of Old Spice, which he apparently applied liberally during his frequent trips to the john. A product of television advertising was Tony, but Melissa insisted he was a specialist in mutual funds and sold more shares to widows than any other independent in the business. Every day after the market closed he appeared at my side to invite me to have an after-work cocktail with him. Always I "demurred politely," in the manner of a properly bred Victorian girl, but on Friday, to his surprise as well as my own, I accepted. Perhaps, J. D., I thought, you can learn something useful from him after he has a few drinks, because you sure haven't learned anything from anybody else.

"Meet me in the parking lot," I said. "At my car. It's a beige Camaro."

"I know it," he whispered. "Mum's the word, hey?"

Melissa was still tidying up her desk when I slipped out of the office, and before I could get my car door unlocked, Tony was walking toward me.

"Want me to drive, baby?" he asked when he reached me.

"No, Papa, you're too old to drive," I replied.

I swung into the traffic on Big Beaver and headed east.

"Where we going, hon?" Tony asked.

"I hear there's a very good piano player with bass at the Colorado Beef House."

"Voo-voo-voo-vroom! There's a helluva lot more at that place."

"You go there often?"

"I been a couple of times. Not cheap but you have to pay for the scenery."

"You mean the pretty waitresses in undress."

"How could I look at them when I'm with a beautiful chick like you? Lisa says you just got divorced, right?"

"Lisa says you've been divorced half a dozen times."

"She's half right. Hey, if God meant for every marriage to succeed, he'd never have invented lawyers."

The Colorado was not as crowded at five-fifteen as it customarily was during lunch, and Nanette sat us at a table a few yards to the right of the piano, where we could see as well as hear the pianist, a slender pale-faced man named Perky Bennett and his bass-viol accompanist, a long girl in her early thirties who seemed never to lift her eyes from the strings she plucked. I was relieved to find that there were several other couples besides Tony and me at the tables. The bar was crowded with as many standees as there were men on bar chairs, but Harry was not among them, although Buford Hickory and his two boys were at their usual location. Tony ordered Crown Royal and water, and I had a Piesporter wine; it was Margarita time, but with a guy like Tony I decided to play it safe.

"Hostess seems to know you," Tony said after we were served. "I bet you worked here once, right?"

"Not right."

"You got the goods to do it, baby, if you wanted to."

"The only thing I want to do right now, Tony, is learn enough about stocks and bonds to get a license and then, maybe, sell half as much as I understand you sell every month."

Blatant flattery is hardly a subtle approach, but it rarely fails with insecure egoists like Tony, and it didn't fail now.

"Hey, know-how is the name of the game. And sex appeal don't hurt neither. Me—I'm the ladies' man. You couldn't sell many women, I don't think, because you're too good looking. But guys you should handle like a magician works with cards."

"Oh? You mean, then, that Melissa deals only with male clients?"

"Lisa! Hell no! Lisa's a technician. She's support staff mainly—works up charts and patterns, junk like that for Harvey to send out in his monthly reports. Oh, she's a smart lady, all right, and she has a few regulars who think she's a brain, but she'd never make it if she had to live off commissions only, like the rest of us do."

"You mean she's paid a regular salary?"

"You better believe it. Eight thou a year if she never sells a piece of paper."

"How do you know that?"

"I know 'cause I'm a snooper, sweetie."

"Well, she must earn it if Mr. Harvey keeps paying her, don't you think?"

"Maybe she does, I don't know. She works like a starving dog smelling a buried bone. But that's because she's got the hots for Harvey."

"Really!"

"Hey—fact! Just watch her sometime when Harvey walks through the office. You'd think she was watching a spaceship take off."

"You certainly keep an eye on people, don't you, Tony. Do you keep tabs on Mr. Skeffin and Peter

Downs and Essie and Mr. Harvey himself, too?"

"Lemme give you a tip, kid, that never goes wrong. You want to get ahead in this world, you better know where the hell you stand at all times."

"I'm not sure I follow you."

"Simple. You watch what other people in your little world are doing so they can't screw you up. Lisa knows that better'n anyone. Like yesterday about noon. You weren't there—you'd gone out to lunch. This guy comes in, little fella wearing a black raincoat—imagine that! A black trench coat like you might see hoods wearing to a Mafia big's funeral in the rain—at least in the movies. You know what I mean?"

"Sure."

"I happen to be on my way out and this guy says to me, 'I want to see Mr. Harvey.' 'He's not in now,' I told him. 'I got a message for him,' he says. Just then Lisa sticks her nose in. She's been listening, see. 'He won't be back till after two o'clock,' she says. 'Can I help you?' Takes the play right away from me, see, as if she was the receptionist 'stead of Essie, who's gone off to the john or someplace. 'I guess so,' the guy says, and he fishes a pack of matches out of his pocket and hands it to her. 'Give him this,' he says. 'He'll know what it means.' And then he turns around and marches off like a KGB agent in a spy movie. So Lisa stole the action from me and she gets the credit for being the busy little bee always on the job when Essie's not at her desk, instead of me. Not a big deal, but it's just a for instance, to show you how people get ahead by keeping their eyes open. You know what I mean?"

"I guess so. But matches! Isn't that a strange way to send a message?"

"Beats me. Probably something Harvey set up in advance. Meet me at some hotel or bar, honey, an' let me know where you are later."

"Oh! You think Mr. Harvey has a girlfriend on the side?"

"Hey—you can't prove it by me. And don't you go telling people I said that!"

"I wouldn't do that, Tony. Really I wouldn't—unless, of course, you try to screw me up on my way to the top."

I feigned a passionate interest in the music of the moment, although I don't think I had the slightest notion then, and certainly none now, of what the duo was playing. I was patching facts together. Someone had left matches for Harvey yesterday; Harry was not at his post today—was there a connection? Why hadn't Harry telephoned me? But suppose the appointment hadn't been for yesterday, but for today? Harry wouldn't have known anything about it until Harvey walked in the Colorado maybe just an hour or so before we had come. So now he would be trailing Harvey, or someone Harvey had talked to, or maybe he had gone to my place to report. I had to get home.

I finished my wine as the music wound down.

"Well, I've got to get home, Tony," I said. "Shall I drop you off at the office?"

"Home! We just got here, woman! I just had one drink!"

"I know, and I'm sorry. I forgot that I'm expecting a long-distance call between five-thirty and six. It's important."

Tony's eyelids slid down to slits as he stared at me.

"Maybe we can have another drink at your place, huh?" he said exploratively—ever the macho egoist.

"Not tonight, lover," I answered with a sweet smile. "Maybe next year."

"Shit! G'wan home then. I'll get a ride back. Don't you worry about that, beautiful!"

I took my leave daintily, with a smile for Nanette as I passed her at the entrance. But outside I got to my car in double time, and going home I was pushing sixty whenever traffic on Big Beaver Road let me. I reasoned that if Harvey had shown up at the Colorado, Harry would try to get a message to me on my telephone tape, and I was right.

It was brief, and his voice was low, almost a whisper into the phone. "Harry at the Colorado Beef House," he said. "Our man just showed. Carries a big brown manila envelope with a label I happened to get a glimpse of while I was walking down the bar to pluck a pack of matches from the ashtray in front of him: Southeast Michigan Assets Company, Incorporated. He ordered a Coke, and when he got a chance said something to Nanette, who went into the back through the kitchen with his message. She returned with Terry, they had a few words, then both went back into the kitchen. I'm waiting and watching. Thirty." Thirty was Harry's way of signing off. His first job as a kid was as a copyboy for the now-defunct Detroit *Times*. Presumably Harry had followed Harvey or whoever had the brown envelope, probably was still waiting and watching somewhere this very minute. But to make sure I phoned Milly.

"No, he's not home yet, Jane," she told me. "He's been pretty regular since he took this job for you, whatever it is, and I'm grateful. I just hope he hasn't gone to the track. It's been almost a year now, and it's sure made a difference. New TV, new mattress and springs, and we're halfway home toward a decent living room suite."

I reassured her, told her he'd just left me a message and he might be quite late, not to worry. I was tired, and I wanted to be available for Harry's next call, so I had a can of soup and a poached egg on toast with a glass of Almaden burgundy. I settled down in front of the TV in my pajamas to watch a National Geographic special on Southeast Asian wildlife, and fell asleep. It was past eleven when I woke. I turned off the telly, and checked my tape just to be sure there had been no calls, though I was certain that the phone's ringing would have awakened me. There had been none. I yawned, and went to bed—to wake at a little past seven to the bluejay shrieking of the telephone.

"Is this J. D. Mulroy?" a familiar voice inquired.

"Speaking."

"Hope I didn't wake you, J. D."

I recognized the voice of Lieutenant James Squires of the Southfield Police Department, with whom I had worked on two stolen jewelry cases.

"That's a vain hope, Lieutenant," I said. "I hope you have a good reason for making my Saturday so early."

"Harry Jenkins," he said.

"What about Harry?"

"I always thought he was Catholic."

"Yes, Harry's Catholic, though God knows when he last went to Mass."

"Then why did they put his body in a Masonic cemetery?"

Homicide cops and morgue attendants develop a black sense of humor. Maybe it's a protective shield. I don't know.

"Harry's dead?" was all I could say.

"Cemetery workers out to sturdy a canopy over an open grave found his body alongside the hole a little over an hour ago. We haven't got the coroner's report yet—doubt we'll get it till late this afternoon, this being Saturday—but it looked like he had a broken neck."

"Has anyone notified his wife?"

"Joe Dougherty did it. Why d'you s'pose I'm calling you? Harry was working a case with you, was he?"

"Helping out a little, yes. Look, Jim . . ."

"Lieutenant Jim, J. D. I'm on duty."

I had the feeling that he was less than half-joking—good homicide cops prefer to find as few bodies in their area of jurisdiction as possible, especially bodies that may compromise friends, so I declined to come up with a smart rejoinder.

"I'm still half asleep," I said. "Let me get myself together with a little toast and coffee, and I'll meet you at the station as soon as I can. Okay?"

There was a considerable pause before he replied.

"You and Harry were pretty close, weren't you?"

"Milly and I were closer."

"Sure. Well, okay. See you soon."

He rang off and left me sinking in a swamp of guilt.

7

A long time ago some smart-alec poet wrote: "Death is a swindler with a smile." Until now I had been passing time, suspecting that the estrangement between Charlotte and Emmett Harvey would turn out to be either another woman, some psychotic hangup, or a financial embarrassment that Harvey could not bring himself to tell his wife about. I doubted that there really was a case for me. Harry's death settled my doubts. In fact, the entire matter now was *my* case rather than Charlotte's or Dr. Mansfield's. I had never been overly fond of Harry, but he was dead because he had been working for me, and I regarded it as my personal and professional obligation to see justice meted out to whoever had killed him. I considered calling Milly, whom I liked a lot, but decided that it was too soon to offer condolences from the one who was, however indirectly, responsible for Harry being dead. I had been swindled, though not in the exact way that poet meant. Instead I called Ahmad, and caught him just before he left his apartment for what he called his karate factory. I briefed him on what had happened.

"Have you considered, J. D., the obvious alternative?" Ahmad asked in his keep-cool voice.

"What?"

"Possible, you know, that somebody killed Harry who has nothing to do with your case. An old grudge, maybe. Another case he was working on."

"He wasn't on any other case."

"That's what he told you. But I've noticed Harry didn't always tell the whole truth."

This was true enough to make me feel a little better. Nevertheless, I asked Ahmad to meet me in Lieutenant Squires's office, and he promised to be there in half an hour. I delayed twenty minutes more to give him time to arrange for a substitute instructor to take over his morning's classes, and then lingered in the corridor just inside the Municipal Building's police entrance off Civic Drive until Ahmad, all six feet eight inches of him, walked in. It was almost an hour since Jim Squires had called, waking me from a sound sleep, but I felt as if I had been playing tennis for three hours and the score was five sets to love in favor of Guilt.

Squires was behind the desk in the tiny cubicle reserved for the homicide officer, which was a part-time job because Southfield doesn't have more than ten or twelve killings a year, and most of those are the result of domestic quarrels and require little investigation. He stared up at the two of us, unsmiling.

"You didn't have to bring your bodyguard, J. D.," he said. "We gave up third degree last month."

Between Ahmad and Lieutenant Squires there existed a rivalry that was ingeniously friendly. Both had been star football players, Ahmad on a championship Rose Bowl–bound Michigan team, Squires on the smaller but also championship Class II Hillsdale College team. Ahmad had continued his sports career with the Miami Dolphins and achieved national fame and substantial wealth courtesy of television; Squires was twenty pounds too light to make it as a linebacker on any professional team, and after college had become a cadet in the Detroit Police Academy. Squires's introduction to Ahmad hardly endeared them to each other. The Steak and Mushroom Restaurant on Ten Mile near Southfield, at that time the busiest intersection in the northwest metropolitan Detroit area, was held up late one

Friday night by two black men, one with a .38-caliber pistol and the other, who stood near the door, with a sawed-off shotgun. The pistoleer was shoveling the night's receipts into a plastic Farmer Jack shopping bag when Ahmad emerged from the men's room slightly behind and to the right of the man with the shotgun. Ahmad has always amazed me with the stealth of his movements. He doesn't seek attention; everything he does, including talking, is done quietly if not quickly. According to the cashier, who had a box seat for the occasion, Ahmad took one step forward, chopped the shotgun wielder in the back of the neck with his left hand, and caught the stock of the shotgun in his right hand with one coordinated movement. So quiet was the event that the pistol-packing money collector did not hear a thing until Ahmad prodded him in the back with the shooting end of the shotgun and said, quietly, "What's happening, brother?"

Squires was a sergeant at the time working the night shift in charge of armed robbery, and in response to the cashier's call he led four policemen into the restaurant, all with drawn weapons, only to find the two bandits, with their arms belt-bound behind their backs, sitting quietly in one side of a booth while Ahmad sat opposite them, with their guns at his side and their ammunition lying harmlessly on the tabletop. Most of the customers had returned to their dinners or drinks, and there was nothing for Squires to do except fill out the details of his report. Just before the robbers were taken outside to the police cars, one of the policemen recognized Ahmad and asked him for his autograph.

"Miss Mulroy's hard hit by Harry's death," Ahmad replied to Squires's taunt. "She asked me to drive along with her here. You want me to wait outside?"

Genial, subservient Ahmad! If the lieutenant wanted to browbeat the little lady who was approaching a hysteria of grief, far be it from Ahmad to interfere; he would absent himself from the scene.

"Naw. You're here already. You knew Harry Jenkins anyway, didn't you?"

"I knew him," Ahmad answered, but he said no more.

"Was he badly beaten?" I asked.

"Not so far as I could see in the spotlights. Way his head tilted over, though, I'd guess his neck was broken. You want to see the photos?"

I did, and I didn't, but I nodded yes.

From a large envelope, Squires produced six eight-by-ten glossies of Harry Jenkins, deceased, shot from various angles and perspectives. The longest view, which must have been snapped from a ten-foot stepladder almost at the side of the body, showed Harry in repose, lying three feet from the open grave. His feet were comfortably apart, his hands clasped across his abdomen, the collar of his sport shirt was neatly tucked outside the neck of his jacket. But the head lolled at a grotesque angle to the right side, as if his neck were made of rubber that had lost its elasticity. The other pictures were shot from various angles, except for two close-ups of the head and shoulders. Squires sat sucking on his briar, which wanted to go out, while Ahmad and I examined the pictures.

"Anything found on the body?" Ahmad asked after he returned the photos to Squires's desk.

"Usual stuff. Wallet—but no cash. Fountain pen. Small change in right trouser pocket. Comb. Small notepad. Kleenex. Nail file."

"Nothing written on the pad?" I asked.

"Nope."

"You checked for impressions on the top sheet that may have come through if Harry had written something on a missing sheet?"

"J. D.," Squires said, "you take the cake for chutzpah! We picked up the body about two hours ago, and you come in here expecting us to have lab and autopsy reports in duplicate all ready for you. If I didn't know you, I'd get downright mean! I definitely will get mean if you ask *me* any more questions. I'm the investigating officer in charge here, you're a citizen who may have information relevant to the case. In fact, you may even be a suspect."

When he made this last remark, he was looking at Ahmad rather than me.

"Now, Jenkins was working for you when he got it, J. D. What was it he was doing for you?"

"He was keeping track of the movements of a couple of people, that's all."

"What people?"

"I can't tell you that without violating the confidence of my client, who is, I might add, a perfectly responsible citizen."

"Who the hell do you think you are—a member of the press? I can make you tell me and you know it!"

"You can make me refuse to tell you in front of a judge and get me charged with contempt of court. That is, if you want to go to all that trouble. Lieutenant, believe me, if I thought telling you the name of my client would in any way help reveal Harry's murderer, I wouldn't hesitate a moment."

Squires tucked the pictures back into their envelope, then leaned back in his chair and knocked his pipe empty into the rubber-edged Oldsmobile wheel cover that had been on his desk ever since I first encountered him three years ago.

"What about you, Dakar? You got anything to say?"

"Seems like the killer has a black sense of humor," Ahmad said, and added after a moment, "I use the term in the theatrical, not in the racial, denotation."

Squires grunted.

"Would seem also, Lieutenant, that he knew about that grave waiting for its rightful owner. Can you see that canopy driving by the cemetery?"

"Yeah. It's about twenty-five yards past the Southfield entrance. Burial was set for yesterday afternoon but it was delayed a day because some relatives had trouble making connections in St. Louis. Grave is in a family plot. Burgemeir. Man to be buried was Ralph Burgemeir. Big muckety-muck in the Masons. Thirty-third degree, whatever that means."

"It means that he gave about as much time to the necessary labors of the Masons as you give to your job, Lieutenant," Ahmad said.

"We don't think there's any connection there. We'll check, of course."

He turned to me again.

"So you flat out refuse to help us in our investigation?"

"If I think of anything that might be helpful, or find out anything I think might help, I'll certainly let you know, Jim," I said, taking a chance with his nickname.

"If you think of anything—fine, tell us. But don't you go mucking around with any investigation of your own, J. D. These aren't society robbers we're looking for, they're cold-blooded killers who like to boast about it. You hear?"

"I hear, Jim."

"You, too, Dakar!"

"Lieutenant," Ahmad said. "I'm just the lady's chauffeur."

It was past nine o'clock when we left the lieutenant's office, outside of which a half dozen people were waiting, and slipped through a side exit into the parking lot. Ahmad had left for Moffat's, and I was already in my car with the motor running before I heard the shouts.

"Wait! J. D.—wait! Wait!"

And who should come huffing and puffing up to the passenger door but Bernie Woodward. His face was red with the exertion of running, and his ink-stained plastic-rimmed spectacles had slipped forward on his nose.

"What's it all about, J. D.?" he asked, sliding into the seat beside me.

"I've no idea what you're talking about, Bernie," I said.

"C'mon now. I saw you go in Squires's office. I was at my desk working up a layout at eight this A.M.— can you believe that? Me at work at eight on a Saturday! But it's got to go in Monday's edition and I shoulda done it yesterday. A guy we use as a local stringer calls the office and tells me Southfield police have found a body in Acacia Cemetery. Which doesn't sound unusual in a literal sense except that it's not buried."

"Does Squires know one of his cops is moonlighting for you, Bernie?"

"So now Squires is talking to you. Two and two. C'mon. You owe me for all that research I did when you were in Florida. Not to mention running down the Colorado Beef House history. It's got something to do with the Beef House, right?"

"Bernie, I know I owe you. But I can't tell you anything because I don't know anything about the murder."

"It was murder, then, not a hit-and-run or accident like thing?"

"Sure, Bernie, it was murder all right. At least that's what Lieutenant Squires thinks. No reason why I can't tell you the name of the victim. It will be in all the evening papers anyway. He was a private investigator named Harold Jenkins."

Bernie's pen was busy now, almost as busy as his tongue.

"And he was working on a case for you, huh? That it?"

"I didn't say that and don't you dare write it. Harry worked for me from time to time, so I knew him, and his wife is a good friend of mine. The lieutenant wanted to get a rundown on Harry, so he called me because he knew I employed him sometimes. That's all I can tell you, Bernie."

"Except his address, of course," Bernie insisted. "And his wife's name. Any children?"

There was no point in not telling Harry's address: Harry advertised in the yellow pages.

"But don't you go round and bother Mrs. Jenkins, Bernie. She's pretty broken up, as you can imagine."

"Cross my heart, I won't do that, J. D. Thanks."

Bernie was as good as his word—but no better. Later, I discovered that he sent a young woman reporter to interview Milly Jenkins, and she did a tearful piece on the anguish of the wife of a private investigator that made a spread on the third page of the Monday *Eccentric*. Reading it, I canceled whatever other debts Bernie Woodward might claim I owed him.

8

In Moffat's, we sat silent in our balcony booth. The restaurant had just opened for the day and the waitresses had not yet taken their stations. It would be another hour before the luncheon crowd began queueing at the reservation desk and polyphonic swells of conversation ascended from the bar and main dining room, like the sound of a distant surf on a windy day. In front of Ahmad was a Jack Daniel's Manhattan, in front of me a Margarita. We sat silent, occasionally sipping our drinks for perhaps a quarter of an hour, before Ahmad decided to say something.

"So," he said, "you figured out our next move yet?"

"Are you volunteering to help me?"

"I got the feeling, Jane honey, that you just might need a little help with this one."

"Uh-huh! Although, it's really a police matter now."

"Sure it is."

"And, as you suggested, Harry's murder may have nothing whatever to do with the case we were working on."

"That's right."

"Even if it is connected, Jim Squires is a damn good cop and he'll probably find the killer p.d.q."

"The quicker the better."

I looked up into Ahmad's eyes directly for the first time since we had sat down.

"Ahmad, there's not much money in it. What I'm trying to recover, according to my client, is her brother-in-law's soul. I'm working for a hundred fifty a day plus expenses."

"I'm not surprised, J. D. Souls come cheap these days. You going to tell me about it?"

I told what there was to tell, which was truly very little.

"Seems like the only thing we have to work from is that telephone tape Harry left you," Ahmad commented when I had finished. "That and the restaurant. How do you think people there would react if I dropped in for a bite and a cocktail or two?"

"Somebody would surely recognize you. A lot of sports buffs hang out there, I'm sure."

"Wouldn't hurt any. Some way you can check up on that envelope Harvey was carrying? Southeast Michigan whatever company?"

"I'll check the accounts files, though I've been looking through them whenever I've had a chance and I don't remember that name."

"Check out the company itself. There's a volume, I think, that lists all stock companies, or most of them, isn't there?"

"Moody's. Industrials, financials, over-the-counter. I'll check on those. What about Harvey? What should I do about him?"

"You didn't mention his name to Squires. I figure you've got a reason."

"I've been watching him for two weeks now. He's hard-working, systematic, decent to his employees— I've got no reason to believe that he had anything to do with Harry's death. I don't want to cause him and his wife and kids a lot of notoriety unless I'm certain he's involved."

"Maybe the coroner's report will tell us something," Ahmad said.

"If Jim will let me have a look at it. You heard him. He practically ordered me to stay out of it."

"Yeah, well, I think I might manage to find out what it says if you can't. One of my best students, Duane Costos, is the son of the medical coroner for Southfield. 'Hi, Dr. Costos,' " Ahmad dramatized. " 'I just called to tell you your boy Doo-wayne is one gung-ho kawan-do karate kid. By the way, I understand you just examined an old friend of mine—Harry Jenkins. I always told Harry he should study karate with me. What killed him?' Words more or less to that effect."

"Worth a try. If I can't find out anything about Southeast Michigan Assets Company, I'll just ask Me-lissa about it. She seems to keep track of every piece of paper that comes in or goes out of the office."

"Tomorrow's Sunday. You got a key to the office?"

"No."

"But the building's open on Sunday, isn't it?"

"It must be. The Troy Tower. Twenty-six stories of attorneys, real-estate operators, doctors, dentists, candlestick makers."

"They probably have a Sunday guard service with a sign-in sign-out routine. Bet I could get in that office with my new little tungsten-hardened needle door lock drill. Want to try?"

"As a last resort, maybe. Let me see whether I can't get a key from Mrs. Harvey. She owes me a little help now if anybody does. God! I wish I'd never heard of her, or that I'd told her big sister this job was beneath my dignity!"

"Yeah gal! You a dignity doll if I evah saw one!" Ahmad said in his imitation-ghetto dialect.

I am not a cruel person. I derive no satisfaction from inflicting discomfort, physical or mental, on another human being. But if inflicting such pain might right a wrong, or aid, however little, in the revelation of truth, I am tough enough to do my duty. Which grand proclamation I make to explain why I did not hesitate one second after entering my apartment-office in dialing the Harveys' home number. If Harvey himself answered the phone, I had decided to ask for Mrs. Harvey; there was no reason to think that he would recognize my telephone voice. In the event, Charlotte answered.

"This is Jane Mulroy," I announced. "If your husband is home, just pretend that I'm a telephone saleslady. Is he home?"

"Yes."

"Within hearing?"

"No. He's upstairs shaving," she whispered.

"Good. Something very serious has happened and I must have your help."

After an instant of very audible silence, Charlotte replied calmly, with a fortitude I didn't expect her to exhibit.

"Of course. What can I do?"

"Do you know where your husband's key ring is right now?"

"Yes."

"Do you know whether he keeps his house key and office key on the same ring with his car keys?"

"Yes, that's right."

"Good. I want you to find an excuse to take his car and meet me at Oakland Mall as soon as you can. Drive to the John R entrance and park as near as you can to the locksmith booth just outside the Sears store."

"I don't know." She lowered her voice. "I have my own car."

"Take his keys by mistake then, and in your hurry forget to return them when you pick up your own. I'll meet you in fifteen minutes."

"Well . . ."

"Fifteen minutes, Charlotte!"

"Yes. Yes, of course."

As I sat in my beige Camaro waiting, and calming myself with a Mozart string quartet on WQRS, I was by no means certain that my command would carry weight. But twenty-five minutes after I had hung up my phone, a gray Escort drew up, hesitated, then as I got out of my car, parked several slots down from me.

"I stopped at Chatham's to get some bologna and milk," Charlotte explained.

"Fine. You had to have a reason for going out, I suppose. You have the keys?"

"Yes."

I held out my hand while she fished in her purse. But when she found the keys, she did not hand them to me.

"Miss Mulroy, I'm not sure I'm going to give them to you. You want to make a duplicate of my husband's office key, and I'm sure you think you have a good reason to do this, but I can't take that responsibility. I mean, Emmett has hundreds of clients and their business is strictly confidential between them and him. Surely you can understand my position."

She was talking herself into the courage to deny me the keys. I'd had no intention of telling her about Harry's death—with her domestic paradise turned into a purgatory, she had enough to worry about—but I needed that key and I meant to get it!

"Charlotte, something has happened that might bring the police into your husband's office and into both of your lives, unless I can discover what they want to know in a matter of hours. I have reason to believe that the answer can be found in a file folder in your husband's office. If I'm right, they won't bother Emmett or you. Trust me!"

She hesitated, then firmed her jaw and straightened her posture.

"Whatever it is, I have a right to know about it. I'm employing you, aren't I?"

"Your sister's employing me."

"Well, I intend to repay her, so that makes *me* your real employer."

What the hell! We had degenerated into an argument in a schoolyard—"You did!"—"I didn't!"—"Did too!"—"Did not!" She wanted the truth, so I decided to give it to her, and if her purgatorial existence moved a little more toward hell, she could blame herself alone.

"All right. I hired a man to watch the Colorado Beef House just in case your husband went there. Those matches we found in his pockets all had a time of day pencilled inside their covers. Friday, another was delivered to him at his office. He went to the Beef House at the appointed time and my man saw him. That's the last he saw of him, however, because he was murdered Friday night. The police want to know who did it, and why. They know he was working for me, but I haven't yet told them who I have been working for, or why. Do you understand now?"

Understanding came slowly—and was followed by shock, then attempted disbelief.

"You don't think for one minute that Emmett would—why, he couldn't kill a cat! We had a kitten once and we wanted to get rid of it but—Miss Mulroy! I think you're making all this up to scare me. That's it, isn't it?"

"Charlotte, the evening papers will tell the story of how Harold Jenkins's body was found in Acacia Cemetery beside a grave that had been dug for another man. Harry was a friend of mine, and he was trying to help me and, though he didn't know it, *you!* I mean to find out who killed him and why. If I can do it without involving you and Emmett, I will. But I'll have to do it in the next twenty-four hours or the police will be knocking on your door. Somehow Emmett's problem is mixed up in this murder. I promise you that!"

"Oh, my God!"

"Will you please give me that key now?"

She handed me the ring.

"Which one is it?"

She pointed to a Dexter dead-bolt special, and I detached it and returned the ring to her.

"Wait for me. It will take only a minute."

Actually, the locksmith needed merely thirty-five seconds to reproduce the key. I returned to where Charlotte stood, and gave her back the original. She stood holding the ring in one hand and the key in the other.

"Does Liz know?" she asked.

"I haven't told the doctor and I suggest that you don't tell her either. Maybe we'll be lucky."

I took the ring and the key from her hands and slipped the key back into its original position.

"I don't know what to do!"

"Go back home and act as if nothing has happened."

"Maybe if I tell Emmett, explain what I was trying to do when I hired you. I only wanted to help him! I wasn't prying!"

I took her arm and began guiding her back to her car. When she was settled in the driver's seat, I closed the door and spoke to her through the opened window.

"Charlotte, Emmett is involved in some dirty business with some vicious people. I doubt that he got into it knowingly, but the fact is that he's stuck now, and if you upset him, he might make a wrong move and he might be killed just as ruthlessly as Harry was. Believe me—the best thing for you to do now is to act as if everything is the same as before you talked with me. Will you try to do that for a day or two?"

I took her silence for assent, although I'm not certain that she understood what I had said. I placed a hand on her shoulder and squeezed gently until she looked up.

"Does Emmett go to the office on Saturday afternoons?"

"Usually, yes."

"You have my phone number?"

She nodded.

"I want you to telephone me as soon as you can after he gets home from the office. Let the phone ring twice, then hang up. You understand?"

"Twice."

"Yes. I'll be waiting for your call. I don't think Emmett is guilty of anything serious, really I don't. I think he's being victimized somehow. Things will work out, Charlotte, if you have patience just a little longer."

"I don't know. I just don't know!"

She appeared to be about to break into sobs, so I snapped her seat belt from the doorpost and held it in front of her.

"Buckle up!" I said brightly. "You don't want to get two tickets if you're stopped for running a red light. And remember, call me!"

I waited until she got her car started and moving slowly out of the parking lot, then I hurried to my Camaro and headed for Moffat's, where Ahmad was waiting for me.

9

The call came at six-fifteen: two rings, then silence. The mid-November dusk showed a rind of gray in the west as Ahmad and I left Birmingham in his burgundy Eldorado, but by the time we arrived at Harvey's high-rise three miles west, it had disappeared. A scatter of office lights winked into the dark above the nearly deserted parking lot, but we marched into the building as if it was five to nine on a Monday morning, me with an underarm leather zip-around paper holder, Ahmad carrying a slender, all-business dispatch case, in which was nothing but a flashlight. I waved a high five to the uniformed attendant behind a miniature desk at the end of the corridor of elevators, telling Ahmad in a loud voice, "I know I left it on my desk— I simply forgot to collect it when I came back from the ladies lounge—you'll see!" We were on our way toward the fifteenth floor before the security guard could stand up, if he wanted to, which I doubt. He came on duty at six but there were still fifty or sixty people in the tower—attorneys putting the final touches on briefs due early Monday morning, finance officers balancing the week's business books, perhaps a psychologist here, and a dentist there. The guard considered his job virtually a sinecure until after nine o'clock, by which hour he would have completed all of the *Free Press* crossword puzzle he was capable of working out.

Before we stepped out of the elevator, Ahmad snapped open his case and took out the heavy-duty rubber-encased flashlight.

"We won't need that," I told him. "There are night lights in the corridors."

"This here's no light, J.D. It's my favo-right unconcealed weapon."

"I hardly think you'll need it one way or the other."

"Hope not. But I've always believed in the Boy Scout motto, and I'm still here to tell you so."

The locksmith had done a perfect job. His key slipped into the lock and snapped back the long dead bolt noiselessly. There was no need for stealth at this hour, so I snapped on the lights, and headed straight for Harvey's office.

"I'll wait out here," Ahmad said, sitting down at Essie's desk, "to receive any guests we might have."

"Be courteous or you'll be fired," I answered.

Harvey's office was as tidy-neat as his closet. I think I'd rather search the premises of a scatterbrain than those of a neatnik. The former is likely to conceal whatever he doesn't want others to find in the first unlikely place he sets eyes on, which is also likely to be one of the first unlikely places you would see. But a person whose systematic mind demands order on display will find a hiding place within a hiding place, so to speak, i.e., within what appears on first examination to be exactly what it is in the proper scheme of things. Acting on this premise, I did not look beneath chairs or under desk drawers or in the toilet tank in the office's private bathroom. Rather, I began a systematic search in the obvious places. The desk revealed nothing one would not expect to find in Harvey's desk, so I moved on to the four-drawer, man-high filing cabinet and worked my way through the *S* filing folders first, then started at the *A*s and ran in twenty minutes or so through the top three drawers to *Z*—Zeller Tool and Die Co. There was no hint of Southeastern Michigan Assets Company.

I had to go down on my knees to get at the bottom drawer, the tag on which read INACTIVES AND CLOSED. It was in this position that Ahmad found me when he came in.

"Must be a tough job—you have to pray for help," he said.

"It's getting to that point," I replied.

The bottom drawer contained, in addition to an electric razor, two divisions: "Inactive" and "Closed." To Harvey's credit, neither was very extensive. In fact, there were only twelve entries in the "Closed" section, and eight of these were marked "Deceased." The "Inactive" file held folders of about thirty accounts, of which Abbott, Richard C., was the first, and Weatherby & Johnson, A Limited Partnership, was the last. I actually passed by the folder I was seeking before my wearied eyes registered what they had seen. The label read S. MG. and the type was of a slightly different face than that on all the others. I handed it up to Ahmad and staggered on numb knees to my feet.

A cursory glance at the contents revealed nothing spectacular: sell and buy confirmation orders with dates and prices.

"I'm going to Xerox everything here and then let's get out," I said. "We can study it at my place."

"Okay, but I sure do want to see how you Xerox on an Hitachi copier."

I had used the machine before for Melissa, and in five minutes I had replaced the file, zipped the copies in my paper case, and was locking the office behind me. As we stepped from the elevator into the lobby, I was haranguing Ahmad: "I told you where we'd find it, didn't I?" The security attendant hardly offered us a glance, for which oversight I was at the moment grateful, though I remember thinking as we were getting into Ahmad's car, If I was the manager of the building, I'd fire that schnook masquerading as a guard.

We sat at my dinette table and examined the sheets in the file. All were photocopies of confirmations of the sales and redemptions of the Redeemable Preference stock of The Southeast Michigan Assets Company, which I summarize as follows:

Emmanuel d'Elessandro, 1371 Hillsport Ave., No. Hollywood, CA 91606
Bought: 2,000 shares @ $1.00 Jan. 2, 1985. Amount $2,000. Commission $42.00

Wilfred J. Tattersby (in transit: will contact.)
Bought: 4,900 shares @ $1.00 Jan. 2, 1985. Amount $4,900. Commission $75.00

Buford T. Hickory, Gold Gate Arms Apartments, Southfield MI 48076
Bought: 1,000 shares @ $1.00 Jan. 2, 1985. Amount $1,000. Commission $22.50

Nancy Ann Garfinkel, 1237 Willow Drive, Troy MI 48098
Bought: 1,000 shares @ $1.00 Jan. 2, 1985. Amount $1,000. Commission $22.50

Terence C. Garfinkel, 1237 Willow Drive, Troy MI 48098
Bought: 100 shares @ $1.00 Jan. 2, 1985. Amount $100. Commission $11.00

Emmanuel d'Elessandro
Redeemed: 2,000 shares @ $100.00 Aug. 15, 1985. Amount $200,000. Commission $750.00

Wilfred J. Tattersby
Redeemed: 1,000 shares @ $100.00 Sept. 5, 1985. Amount $100,000. Commission $550.00

Buford T. Hickory
Redeemed: 250 shares @ $100.00 Sept. 5, 1985.
   Amount $25,000. Commission $125.00

Nancy Ann Garfinkel
Redeemed: 100 shares @ $100.00 Sept. 5, 1985.
   Amount $10,000. Commission $75.00

Terence C. Garfinkel
Redeemed: 10 shares @ $100.00 Sept. 5, 1985.
   Amount $1,000. Commission $11.00

"Make any sense to you?" Ahmad asked.

"I don't know. D'Elessandro owned the Colorado Beef House before it was sold to the present owner, Terence Garfinkel."

"Oh? One hundred and ninety-eight thousand dollar capital gain! Bet this stock was part if not all of the payment for the place. Who's Buford T. Hickory?"

"Buford T. Hickory is B. T. A nattily dressed walrus of blubber who spends most of his afternoons in the Beef House with two bodyguards. He has a crush on the night bartendress who goes by the name of Lorelei."

Ahmad was silent for a few moments, then said, "If that stock is really worth a lot, might be old B. T. was a silent partner with d'Elessandro, and these thousand shares are his payoff."

"I thought a bar ownership license had to list all owners."

"Owners proper, sure. But what if d'Elly borrowed money from B. T. to buy the bar in the first place? B. T. could have held a mortgage on the place, or a note with a lien on the building. Lots of ways to avoid having your name on a license and still have a piece of the place. Probably your counsel can check that out for you."

"I hate to bring Ed into this."

"You don't get the right answers pdq, he'll be defending you in court on charges of obstructing justice."

"You really think Jim would do that to me?"

"I don't think he'd have any choice. He's got to run down every lead, and you're concealing one that might be important, 'specially if he's getting nowhere with what else he's got."

"You're right, as usual. Well, in a way Ed's already in it. Maybe he won't mind too much."

"Sho. Pahdners in crime. Good preface to partners in marriage. Reverse of the usual order."

"Terence C. Garfinkel," I deliberately mused out loud, ignoring what Ahmad thought of as a joke. "You know, the manager of the Beef House is called Terry. D'you suppose he could be this Garfinkel?"

"Shouldn't be hard to find out. Give 'em a ring and ask for Terence Garfinkel."

"You do it," I said, and tossed him a package of paper matches with the telephone number printed on it. "I like to study your technique."

Ahmad dialed, and after fifteen seconds got an answer.

"I should like to speak to Mr. Terence Garfinkel, your manager, ma'am, if he's available at the moment."

After a thirty-second wait, Ahmad hung up the phone.

"The very same Garfinkel, J. D. And now we come to Nancy Ann. His wife? His sister? His mother?"

"Aunt maybe. Or first cousin," I continued the game.

"Three-to-one his wife," Ahmad said.

"I'd better call Ed and get him working on our problems."

"It's ten-thirty, J. D. Nothing he can do at ten-thirty on Saturday night unless he's got duplicate keys to a lot of offices in Lansing. Or you do, which wouldn't surprise me. 'Course, you can talk to him, but I'd just as soon not be here when you do."

He got up and slung his five-foot-long Burberry all-weather coat over his shoulders, like a Hollywood portrayal of a European count about to make an exit.

"Keep in touch," he said, and left.

I thought a while before I dialed Ed. He answered on the third ring.

"Wake you?" I asked.

"Maybe."

There was a brief silence.

"Don't you know?"

"You lonely, honey? Want me to come over?"

"No, I'm worn out. I wondered whether you'd like to come over for coffee and eggs in the morning."

Another several seconds of silence.

"Got a problem with your case, huh?"

"What a nasty thing to say! Don't you have any confidence in your charm anymore?"

"Lots. I've had four invitations to breakfast tomorrow from various ladies. Unfortunately, none for tonight. But you got a problem, right?"

"I'll tell you about it in the morning. Nine o'clock okay?"

I like Ed Rogers. He is intelligent, well-proportioned, generally sweet-tempered, tolerant of my changing moods, has enough Irish in him to kick over the traces of reality from time to time, and I think his first wife Helen was crazy not to hold on to him. Someday, I expect, I'll marry him. We have taken two three-week holidays together, living as husband and wife and getting along comfortably in the tedium of touring as well as in the excitement of sex. But he has this thing about raising a family, for which I have no enthusiasm. Not now. Nor in the foreseeable future. I don't hate children, or dogs for that matter, but I prefer both at a distance. Children are demanding of your time and emotions, and dogs, despite their friendliness, are dirty. Some children I know are both demanding and dirty.

I can do without them, and unless some overwhelming maternal instinct sweeps me into its vortex, I shall do without dogs or children of my own for the rest of my life. All of which I write to explain why Ed and I aren't married now, and why I'm not sure we'll ever be. But you never can tell; someday he might change his mind about having a family of his own.

Ed has one trait which does not endear him to me: he tends to be pre-prompt, i.e., early for appointments—at least with me. He tells me to meet him at a certain intersection at five o'clock, it's raining eels and fishes, so I time myself to step out of the taxi at precisely five o'clock to find him, damp as a dunked doughnut, and he greets me with some such question as, "Where've you been, honey? I've been standing here fifteen minutes." But it's a forgivable fault, as I infer from it that he's eager to see me.

This Sunday morning was no exception. I was just setting the breakfast table when the lobby buzzer sounded; it was twelve minutes before nine. The first few flakes of the millions to come this winter were pirouetting in front of my broad living room window on their way down to the street when I opened the door to let Ed in.

"Winter is a-comin' in. Lhoude sing god-damn!" he sang out in imitation of Ezra Pound.

The few flakes on the shoulders of his coat melted as he leaned forward to kiss me, and for a moment I had to fight off a wave of depression, which swept over me without warning—snowflakes dissolved by a change of climate, Harry alive one hour, dead the next, Milly happy with her new bed one day, lying grieving on it the following day.

"Are you all right, Jane?" Ed asked, sensing my distress.

I hugged him a little harder, a little longer than he had any right to expect, and the montage of images in my head dissolved into their proper frames.

"I'm okay," I assured him. "It's just that I get the shivers thinking about winter."

"You'd prefer the Florida seaside, would you?"

"I've had enough of Florida for a while, too. You're early, as usual, and you'll just have to entertain yourself while I whip up an omelette. Sit down and have some coffee."

I had already diced a quarter of a green pepper and sliced spaghetti-thin strips of Swiss cheese, so all I had to do really was whip up five eggs with a tablespoon of cream, a couple shakes of garlic salt, and a generous tablespoon of hearty port wine, then fold it into the omelette pan sizzling with melted butter. When the mix was nearly tight in the pan, I sprinkled the pepper bits on top and crisscrossed the cheese strips over all, then neatly folded the circle into a half pie and turned off the heat. I have never met a man who did not swear my omelette is the best he ever tasted, and I never expect to meet one.

After we had eaten more than half the meal, Ed looked up at me and said, "Okay, let's hear it."

"Are you sure you want to get involved, darling?"

"Don't tease. This has got to be serious or you wouldn't want to involve me. You're in a jam, right?"

"Right."

"With the law, of course."

"Who else?"

"Tell me."

I had decided to hide nothing from him, as much for his own protection as an attorney as for my own, so I began at the beginning with Dr. Mansfield's call, and ended by handing him the copy of the Southeastern Michigan Assets Company's file folder. He never interrupted my recitation, though I paused several times, ostensibly to eat but really to give him a chance to ask questions. He would have made as good a psychiatrist as a lawyer.

"If Jim Squires insists I tell him who my client is, and what I was doing for her, will I have to tell him, Ed? After all, he's not a judge."

"No, and you're not a newspaper reporter who can claim fourth-estate privileges either. Jane, dear! This isn't a misdemeanor Jim's dealing with! It's murder— the major felony of murder! You're obliged to help Jim. It's your duty as a citizen!"

I nibbled on a piece of toast.

"If I refuse?"

"He can hold you as a material witness. But you're not going to refuse. You're going to tell him whatever you know about the matter."

"All right, your honor. But I don't have to mention Dr. Mansfield, or Mr. and Mrs. Harvey, do I? Can't I just tell him that Harry was watching the Beef House on my orders, and so far as I know he was there Friday afternoon?"

"No way! You can leave out the doctor, or leave it to Mrs. Harvey to mention her sister if she wants to, but you've got to let Jim have that telephone tape, because it may be Harry's last words. And you've got to give him this copy of the file you stole. Both may be material clues in the solution of the crime. God, Jane! The law was developed for the protection of honest citizens. And if you would take the trouble to obey it, you wouldn't get in jams like this!"

"Ed, I called you for advice, not for a lecture. I thank you for the advice, and I guess I'll follow it if I have to. But what I really called you for concerns this file. Southeastern Michigan Assets Company, Inc. What does an assets company do?"

"Handles money for people, as a rule. Makes investments for them in real estate, maybe short-term bonds, whatever, to bring the investors a high rate of return. The good ones do that. The bad ones go broke, or claim to."

"Okay. So this one is incorporated. That means exactly what?"

"That means they have properly requested incorporation under the laws of the state in which they chose to incorporate, and have supplied the facts required for incorporation approval."

"The Southeastern Michigan Assets Company would probably be incorporated in Michigan, wouldn't it?"

"Probably, but not necessarily. Tax considerations, disclosure requirements, other factors lead a lot of corporations to go to Delaware or some other state where procedures are minimal."

"Okay. Let's pretend I want to set up a corporation in Michigan. How do I go about doing it?"

"Well, you file at the Corporation Bureau in Lansing. There's a form, of course."

He paused and closed his eyes, organizing his memory.

"You will have to state the name of the proposed corporation; its purpose or purposes; the number and the classes of the shares to be authorized; the name or names of the original incorporators; and the address of the initial registered office."

"That's all?"

"Essentially. Pay the fee, of course. Fourteen dollars now, I think."

"I checked through Standard & Poor's guide, and Moody's corporation directories, but I couldn't find this company."

"Okay, so they're not a public company. The stock is privately held."

"There's no directory for such private companies?"

"Jane, there are hundreds of thousands of private companies in the country. They come and go like clouds on a windy day. By the time you got such a directory ready for publishing in even one state, it would be forty percent inaccurate."

"So how do I find out who the incorporators of Southeastern Michigan Assets are?"

"Easy. Go to Lansing and look it up in the files. They're open to the public."

"Couldn't I just call somebody there and save myself a trip?"

"You happen to have a friend in that bureau?"

"I thought *you* might. *Hoped* you might."

Ed sipped some coffee and his eyes settled, unseeing, on the butter tray.

"Well," he said after a time, "Shawn Dougherty is a counsel in the Attorney General's office now. I suppose he could check it out for me if I asked him to. I don't know that I want to, though."

"Don't tease me now," I said edgily, but looking into his eyes I realized that he wasn't teasing.

"Jane, you know I love you, don't you?"

"I know, and because you love me I expect you to help me if you can."

"I want to, honey. But the best way I can help you, I think, is not to let you get any more deeply involved in this mess than you are now. That's why I'm suggesting that we call Jim Squires right this minute and go see him at his office, or his home, if necessary, this being Sunday. He lives just off Civic Center Drive, no more than ten minutes from here. Tell him what you've told me and let him work it out. That's his job. You'll be in the clear."

"And what about Charlotte and Emmett Harvey? And the doctor?"

"If they're involved in this murder, which I doubt, they should be dragged over the coals. If they're not, no great harm will be done. Jim isn't going to tell the press boys all he knows."

"Maybe not, but he'll want to talk to Emmett Harvey, and then Emmett will know that his wife hired me to investigate him and the doctor will know that I can't be trusted with a confidence. Uh uh, no way am I going to tell all to Father Squires, unless my life depends on it."

"You can't be serious!"

"Deadly!"

"Damnit all, Jane. You hold that attitude long enough and your adverb may become an adjective. You just don't seem to comprehend what has happened to your friend Harry. Apparently he really did discover something that was dangerous to whatever mob is involved with that Colorado Beef House, and they killed him. Repeat: *killed, murdered!* What do you think they'll do to you if you keep poking around and come close to discovering the same thing? Let Jim Squires do the investigating. He's getting paid for it, has the manpower and the resources to do the job. It's quite possible, likely even, that your clients aren't involved in the murder. What Harry found probably has nothing to do with them at all."

"I hope you're right about that."

"Then you'll come with me to see Jim?"

"No."

Ed slammed his fist down on the tabletop, rattling the cups in their saucers.

"All right," he said, "I'll go see him myself."

"You can't without my permission. You're my lawyer and you can't violate the confidence of your client any more than I can."

"Shows how much you know about the law. A lawyer is obliged to assist in the pursuit of justice if information concerning the commission of a crime is revealed to him."

"Okay, but you still can't go."

"Why not?"

"Because you love me, and I'll never speak to you again if you do."

I wasn't smiling when I spoke, and Ed glared across the table at me for five full seconds. I glared right back at him. Finally, he shook his head slowly and sighed in defeat.

"All right. I'll call Shawn first thing in the morning and get him to look up the incorporation application. I should have the information by noon if he's not out of the capital. Where can I get in touch with you if you're not in jail? At Harvey's office?"

"I'll be there. What do you want to do today?"

"Forget this whole conversation."

"Want to take a drive in the country and watch the last leaves fall?"

"Not particularly."

"Drive over to the Franklin Cider Mill and have some doughnuts and cider?"

"I just ate, woman!"

"Want to go to the moom-pitchurs and watch Bo Derek make love to Sylvester Stallone, or Woody Allen, or some other great stud?"

"Definitely not."

"Want to go to bed and make love to little ole me?"

"A farewell gift, is it?"

"Are you taking a trip?" I asked, all innocence.

We cleaned up the breakfast dishes, then both took the trip that only willing and eager lovers can enjoy.

10

"So when I got in my car, the moon was halfway up the sky, not a cloud anywhere 'round, shank of the evening, and I sure didn't feel like hitting the sack with a Sunday morning snooze coming up, so I thought, Why not have myself a couple of cocktails and a hefty hunk of prime rib, since I didn't have any dinner on account of somebody wanting me to help her rob a broker's office. Next thing you know, I'm sitting at the bar in the Colorado Beef House out past John R— you know where that is, J. D.?"

Ahmad and I were sitting in a booth at Zimm's Family Restaurant a few blocks down Woodward from my apartment. Heavy frost had meringued the rooftops all over town, and we both wore topcoats. It was a few minutes past eight on Monday morning, and I sensed a glumness on the faces of everyone in the restaurant, bolting down their breakfasts because they realized the finality of winter's approach. The splendid Indian summer had seemed capable of drifting on endlessly, but this morning's rind of frost on exposed car windows and roofs, coupled with the almost rhythmic spurts of wind that sandpapered your cheeks, left no doubt about autumn's demise.

"Lively little place, that is 'long about midnight on a Saturday. They have a lady trio on the bandstand— piano, bass, and clarinet, and those skinny chicks can belt out first-rate New Orleans jazz, or drag a blues that makes you want to cry. Three R's they call themselves: Rita, Ruby, and Rosalind. You s'pose those are their real names, J.D.?"

"Not likely," I answered patiently, waiting for Ahmad to get started with his story.

His narratives, like his athletic accomplishments, require a proper warm-up period. There was no sense in trying to hurry him, so I sat sipping my coffee and wondering whether anything he might say would discourage Jim Squires from charging me with obstructing justice.

"Being the shy violet that I am, naturally I sit at the far end of the bar up against the wall, kinda so I can see everybody but nobody has to see my ugly black kisser les' they want to. Come to *thank* of it, I do believe I was the only black dude in the place."

"Were there any Chinese?" I asked. "Or Eskimos?"

"One of the waitresses, tiny little thing, is half and half I think. Myrna her name is."

"As in Loy?"

"Right. She was born in Frisco, she told me. Said her father owns a piece of a place called The Dragon's Tongue."

"Ahmad, please!"

"Right. So here I am holding down one end of the bar, and in about the same position half a mile up at the other end is this sumo wrestler in a chamois sport jacket, and would you believe it? We're both drinking Manhattans, except mine is on a Jack Daniel's base. Don't know what he was using."

"Mr. B. T. Hickory," I commented, and was ignored.

"You know how you get the feeling that people are staring at you? 'Course, I'm used to it being big as I am, but I mean when the novelty is over and you still have that feeling? Beautiful girl like you must know what I mean, the world being loaded with voyeurs of both sexes. Well, after maybe ten minutes I'm gettin' tired of being the ape in the cage, so I start staring right back at the other end of the bar, never blinking more than once in ten seconds, and pretty soon Big Bear leans over to Little Bear, says something in his ear, and this little twerp sashays down the bar to where I am—standing on tiptoe he didn't come up to my shoulder when I'm sitting. 'You Ahmad Dakar?' he asks.

" 'Maybe,' I reply. 'Who wants to know'?

" 'If you are, Mr. Hickory would like for you to join him for a drink.'

" 'Hickory the fat man was sitting next you?'

" 'Right.'

" 'You tell Hickory he wants to set up a table someplace, I'll have a drink with him.'

" 'You can have my seat other end of the bar.'

" 'Don't you hear good, little man?' I say, bearing down a bit now.

"He squints tough at me, but then he strolls on back up the bar and gives my message. Whole thing makes me think of the Ruskies and our people debating the shape of the nuclear discussion table, and I'm hoping that more comes out of this discussion than came out of that one."

Ahmad stopped talking and took a long sip of coffee.

"Did it?" I asked.

"Hard to tell this point in time, as the politicos like to say. You can tell better than me anyway. Hickory works himself out of his bar stool after a bit, calls little Myrna over to him, slips her a bill with his left hand and a rub-a-dub-dub on her butt with his right, and points to a table for four off in the middle of the room. Then he waddles over there with his messenger right behind, plops down in a chair the little guy holds out for him, and waves to me. I'm in no hurry, so I take my time finishing up my drink, then studying my check before I put a sawbuck on it and wait for my change. Bartender, a busty blonde weighing a hundred and a half with all the pounds in the right places, says to me, 'Mr. Hickory has already paid your bar tab, sir.'

"I leave her a buck for good will and amble over to Mr. Hickory's table. 'B. T. Hickory, Dakar,' he says. 'I do believe I've seen every game you ever played in Detroit. You never made it to the Silverdome, did you?' Now Myrna minces in with a round of drinks—she got my order from the bartender but very politely inquires in her furry bunny voice before she puts it down in front of me, 'Manhattan—Jack Daniel's, isn't it?'

" 'No, I never did,' I answer Hickory's question. 'I retired the year after it went into operation, and we didn't schedule the Lions that year.'

"Hickory hasn't introduced the little guy, so I turn to him and say, 'Don't believe we've met before, have we?' Before he can answer, Hickory says, 'This here's Tim Leary. Works for me.' He takes half his Manhattan down in one swallow. 'Read a piece in the paper about you a month or so ago. You're teaching kids judo, or something, it said. Keepin' them off the streets.'

"It was an article by Frank Perkins, a *News* sportswriter who does features from time to time in a Sunday column entitled 'Where Are They Now?' Frank takes you out to lunch, gets you high on compliments and reminiscences if the drinks don't do it, then slips you a series of questions about your business life, if any; your hobbies, hatreds, political affiliations, golf handicap—whatever. I figured the write-up would help advertise my school, and it did. But I don't figure old Blubber Boy is interested in my good works, so I say, 'When the big dough stops rollin' in, guy's gotta pick up bucks wherever he can.'

" 'Very true, very sad but very true,' B.T. agrees. 'I don't guess you pick up too many bucks teachin' kids self-defense, though. I'd guess you get a lot of satisfaction out of it, doing good for youngsters and for the community, too, but you can't spend the rewards of charitable endeavors, can you?'

" 'I get by,' I say, realizing now that he's working me around to some proposition or other.

" 'Tell me, Dakar—if you don't mind my asking— are your hours, your teaching hours that is, adjustable?'

" 'Adjustable?' I repeat after him, acting dumb.

" 'Yes. I mean, if you were offered a second job, let's say, in the afternoons and evenings, could you adjust your teaching to the morning hours? Before one P.M?''

" 'Hell, man, I do most of my work in the morning now. A few evening classes Tuesdays and Thursdays, but most in the morning. What're you getting at, Hickory?'

" 'I'll come right up front with you, Dakar. No use wasting your time or mine. I need a muscle man. You sure look to me like you could fill the bill.'

"I stare at him quite a while, then sip at my drink as I appear to be considering the offer. 'Somebody out to reshape your face, Hickory?' I ask.

" 'I've got a few enemies wouldn't mind giving me a new look, sure. Who hasn't? But it's nobody in particular. I'm a night owl, see. Close up this place sometimes, a couple other places time to time. I like to play a little high-stake poker once in a while, and I carry a wad with me just in case a game develops. You know what I mean?'

"I know what he means, and nod my understanding.

" 'Those kind of hours aren't the best for keeping me in shape for my work,' I say. 'Couple of nights a week, sure. Fridays and Saturdays wouldn't bother me, but if you're talkin' five, six nights running, I couldn't do it. Money I'd gain from you I'd lose in my business. You can't fool kids very long if you're not in shape, man.'

" 'Maybe you could adjust your hours some. Say, move your earliest classes up to ten, even eleven. That'll get you six hours shut-eye. Ought to be enough for a grown man, 'specially since we're talking only four nights a week.'

"I sip and think a while.

" 'I'm talking a thousand a week, Dakar. Adds up during the year, and I don't report it to IRS or Social Security either.'

" 'Uh-huh. Mighty tempting offer.'

" 'One other thing. You drive my car, and you call me Mr. Hickory.'

"I snap to attention. 'Mr. Hickory,' I say in my deep-down tone of voice, 'you want a chauffeur, you hire some dumb honky to do your driving. I don't wear a chauffeur's uniform for no-buddy! You dig?'

" 'Who said anything about a uniform? Listen, Dakar, I want you to drive because I'm too fat to be comfortable behind the wheel of a car, and too drunk late at night. Tim here—he's my lookout, but he can't watch the road and the roadside at the same time.'

" 'What's he watching for?' I ask. 'Rabbits, squirrels to pot with that peashooter he's packin'?'

" 'You noticed that! Good! I like a man keeps his eyes open all the time. He carries it to protect me. He's got a permit, and like I say, I often carry a good stake with me. No sense in taking chances with the Saturday-night-special banditos, is there?'

"I sip a little, think some, then sip some more, and finally I say, 'I don't know what you do, Mr. Hickory, but I know that money has to come from someplace. It don't sprout on bushes or fall like manna from heaven. But numbers and drugs make big bucks. I want no connection with those operations directly or indirectly through you. You don't have to tell me where you get your bread, it's none of my business, but if you tell me you're gonna hire me, I'm gonna assume that you have no dealings with bookies and pushers. Just tell me you can't use me if that assumption is wrong, and I'll thank you for the drink and be on my way.'

"He sits there overflowing his chair like a Buddha in modern dress, and a little smile creeps over his lips, pushing the flushed peaches of his cheeks up almost into his eyes. Then he turns to Tim and says, 'I like this man, Timmy boy. He didn't go through college for nothing. He lays out the terms of his contract like a lawyer before he's going to sign on the team.' He turns to me then. 'Dakar,' he says, 'I'm offering you the job and I'm telling you my money comes from income on investments that are perfectly legal. That is, what I don't make playing cards. I'm good at that, as you'll soon see. What about it?'

" 'Thousand a week?'

" 'Right. Every Saturday night.'

" 'Cash?'

" 'Cash.'

" 'When you want I should start?'

" 'Tuesday. Meet me here at one P.M.'

" 'All right, Mr. Hickory. I'll give it a try for a week or two. You don't like my work, say so and I'm history. And if I got no complaints, you can count on me to keep the bugs off you.'

"And that, J. D., is the story of how I came to be added to Mr. B. T. Hickory's payroll. Also, how I come to be faced with my present moral dilemma."

Ahmad's expression was deadly serious, so I knew he wasn't.

"Which is?"

"Well, I'm working for you, right?"

"Right."

"But I'm also working for Hickory."

"Right."

"But the Good Book says, 'No man can serve two masters . . . God and mammon.' "

"So?"

"Well, I'm just hoping that God's a woman!"

I acknowledged his little joke with a glance toward the ceiling, a gesture asking forgiveness from the true deity, a plea for tolerance toward those who know not what they say.

"You know, this might be dangerous work," I said. "I don't like the looks of Tiny Tim. Want to borrow Snubby—just in case?"

"You know I'm dead set against guns, J. D."

"I know, but I don't want you dead because you're set against them."

"Ooooo! I'm gonna steal that pun!" Ahmad marvelled.

"I almost hope there's nothing wrong with big B. T., that he's just an overgrown playboy and that he won't lead us anywhere. If that's how it is, how much of your weekly grand do I get? Half?"

"Another moral dilemma!" Ahmad said, picking up our breakfast check. "Call it square if I take care of this whole thing?"

"Deal."

My own moral dilemma bothered me through the rest of the day, as I plied my new trade at Harvey's office. I hadn't mentioned to Jim Squires that I was in training, so to speak, at a brokerage office, but I truly expected when I went home to hear his voice on my telephone tape demanding that I appear in his office "pronto," which was one of his favorite words. There seemed clearly to be a connection between the Southeast Michigan Assets envelope that Emmett Harvey had brought to the Colorado Beef House and Harry's murder, because apparently, it was the last thing Harry was concerned with before he was killed. I was definitely interfering with the investigation of the murder by not telling Jim about it, not giving him my copies of the company's file. Jim was entitled to all the pieces of the puzzle, even if some didn't fit, which is to say even if that file had nothing to do with the murder. I knew that I would convince myself to give it to him, along with the marked matchbooks, before the day was ended, yet I delayed as long as I could, even having a drink with Melissa after work at the Little Foxes. She was concerned about the boss.

"He seems to be depressed," she confided to me. "He doesn't laugh or even smile the way he used to do."

"Perhaps he's ill," I said.

"I don't think so. You know what I think? I think he's having trouble at home."

"But you told me he was a devoted family man."

"He was—still is, I'm sure. But things can change between a man and his wife, as you and I know from experience. You come in the office late so you wouldn't notice, but for a couple of months now he's been coming in earlier than anybody and staying on later. He didn't used to be like that. No, I'm sure there's something wrong at home."

Her tone of voice was by no means doleful as she uttered this conclusion, and the gleam in her eye was close to predatory. I remembered a wailing refrain from a down-South blues song: "Come home to mama, baby, and everything will be awl-right!"

"If Mr. Harvey got ill, I mean had to go to the hospital for a month or more, who would take over the operation of the business?" I asked.

The question startled her. Obviously she had not thought about this possibility.

"Well, I don't know," she said. "I don't think he's physically ill."

"Continued depression as often as not leads to real physical illness and requires hospital treatment," I pointed out authoritatively. "That's why so many psychiatric wards are overcrowded."

"Well, I guess he would appoint someone to look after the business."

"If it was me," I said, "I'd appoint you, Melissa."

"Oh!"

"Don't you think you could do it?"

"Well, yes, I could do it, I think."

"Sure you could. I bet you know the facts about almost every account that's ever gone through the office."

"Actually, I have handled just about all of them in one way or another through the years. Yes, I'm sure I could do it! But I hope to God I never have to!"

"Oh, that reminds me. I meant to ask you last week. Someone phoned and asked about the price of a local company stock I never heard of. You weren't in at the moment, so I asked Al and Tony but they never heard of it either. By the time I got back to the telephone the caller had rung off."

"What was the company?"

I puckered my forehead, trying hard to remember.

"Southwest—no—Southeast Michigan something or other. Let me think."

I thought, then had a revelation.

"Southeastern Michigan Assets Company. Yes, I'm sure that was it."

She thought a few moments now.

"Are you certain that was the name?"

"It was something pretty close to that. I checked our files, of course, and the directories, but there was no record of it."

"Well, the reason for that is we've never handled it. Take my word for it, because I never heard of it."

I took her word, and a few minutes later left for home to make the call I hated to make. Jim had recorded no message on my telephone tape, and his silence somehow seemed more minatory than any verbal threat might have been. As I dialed the Southfield Police Station, I was hoping that the switchboard sergeant would tell me that Lieutenant Squires had gone home for the day, or was in conference and couldn't be disturbed. I had no such luck.

"One moment, please," he said, and I heard Jim's line ringing.

His voice seemed unusually cheery as he called "Hello" through the wire. I decided to respond in kind.

"Hi, Jim, J. D. Mulroy here. I'm ready to confess!"

"J. D.! Hey, your underground wastes no time spreading the news, does it? Who told you? Bernie Woodward, I bet."

Hold the horses, J. D., common sense commanded. Time to reconnoiter and reassess—but not confess!

"I didn't get the full details. Fill me in if you've time, will you?"

"He's a known racetrack bum and gambler. Ricky Janescu. Probably took Harry for a bundle, or maybe it was the other way round. Anyway, apparently there was a showdown between them, and Ricky, who used to be a prizefighter, clobbered him. Doc Costos says he whacked Harry in the neck with something pretty heavy—tire iron, maybe, or a baseball bat, and it was lights out for Harry. Sorry if I bothered you, J. D., but you know we've got to track all leads."

"You didn't bother me any, Jim. Glad you got it cleared up."

I hung up and sat in stunned relief for several minutes before I began to try to piece it all together.

11

By eight o'clock Monday evening, I had narrowed the possibilities to two alternatives: either the murder was in fact, as Jim Squires had concluded, the violent ending of a quarrel over a gambling debt; or the real cause behind Harry's murder was being covered up by the charge against Ricky Janescu. In other words, either Janescu was the murderer, or he wasn't and was being framed. You would have made a wonderful weather-person, J.D., I thought. It definitely will rain tomorrow, unless it is absolutely clear.

I called Ed, intending to brief him and solicit his opinion. "Jim has charged a man named Janescu with Harry's murder," I told him as a prologue to the recapitulation of my reasonings.

"I know," he said.

"How d'you know?"

"Same way everyone else knows by now. I read the Monday *Eccentric*. Don't you?"

"It's in the paper already?"

"Front page, lower right. Byline: Bernard Woodward."

I don't know why I should have been surprised. I had known that Bernie was on the case, and I knew him well enough to know that he wouldn't drop a story that had already taken up some of his time.

"I'm glad it's over," Ed said. "You were getting downright neurotic about protecting your client, and I was beginning to wonder whether you were really going to hide something serious from Jim."

"Of course I was," I replied, more testily than necessary. "And I'm still mad at him. He scared me into telling you about my client, and now I feel like an unprofessional idiot."

"But a beautiful idiot," he soothed. "A kissable idiot, a very lovable idiot."

"But not a saccharinely silly one. Night-night, confidant."

Five minutes later I had a copy of Monday's *Eccentric* from the box outside the building lobby. The story was brief and had obviously been the last item worked into the front page format. No doubt it had been tailored to replace the one originally scheduled for that space.

BOXER CHARGED WITH CEMETERY MURDER

Ricky Janescu was arrested early this morning and charged with the murder of Harold Jenkins, whose body was discovered beside an open grave in Acacia Cemetery Sunday morning.

Janescu, known as Bulldog Janescu, was ranked sixth among middleweight contenders by *Ring Magazine* twelve years ago.

Homicide Lieutenant James Squires of the Southfield Police Department says both men were known racetrack bettors and speculates that the killing may have concluded an argument over a gambling debt.

The discovery of a cigarette lighter belonging to Janescu found in Jenkins's trouser pocket led police to Janescu. Hairs suspected to belong to Jenkins, as well as filaments of cloth matching a tear in Jenkins's trousers, were found in the trunk of Janescu's car.

Janescu is expected to stand mute upon ar-
raignment tomorrow afternoon.

"An open and shut case to all appearances," Ahmad
commented when I phoned him later in the evening.
He had already read the newspaper account. "Gets you
off the hook."

"It does that, doesn't it?"

"So now you can forget all about it."

"I could do that, couldn't I?"

"Uh-huh. Or—you could get an Aeroflot plane to
Moscow and have a little tête-à-tête with Comrade
Gorbachev."

"But I won't, will I? You know what I've been
thinking?"

"Same thing I been. How come, night after Harry's
body is found, I'm hired to take Janescu's place."

"Right! Of course, it could be coincidence, I suppose.
B.T. fired Janescu, putting him in a bad mood. Later
he meets Harry, they quarrel."

"Could be. But where was Harry Friday night? And
when did Big Boy fire Janescu?"

"Or maybe never?"

"Right. Think you can find out, J.D?"

"I mean to try."

"How?"

"I'll ask Janescu."

"I never thought of that. Keep in touch."

I took a deep breath after I hung up the phone,
closed my eyes, and lay back in my easy chair, trying
to induce the calm of the first stage of transcendental
meditation. Things had been moving too fast, sweeping
me along in their stream so that I had a confused
perspective. I needed time now to empty my mind of
emotions, allow me to focus events and people as a
motion picture operator might focus his lens's projec-
tion to the proper distance from the theater screen.

In this state I do not think, and I'm not sure whether I feel—certainly not in any conventional way of peace, joy, melancholy, apathy. Rather, a sense of spiritual apartheid separates the body and its functions, stilling them somehow so that there is a separate entity of You that is pure Mind, Spirit, or Soul, if you prefer. Pulse slows, pressures fade, things (yourself included) merge toward the Universal Oneness That Is.

Mumbo jumbo? Autohypnosis? Only to those who have not succeeded in achieving (usually because they have not seriously tried to achieve) that true separation of Body and Spirit that revitalizes both. In this state, Time simply does not exist: five minutes or five hours are indistinguishable from each other.

The telephone's ringing gradually brought me back to the reality of my Body's world. Twenty-five minutes had passed since Ahmad and I had talked. Hazily, I picked up the receiver and breathed "hello" into it.

"Where were you?" Ed's voice inquired, anxious-angry. "I was about to ring off." And when I did not instantly answer, he added, "Not in the shower, I hope."

"No. Not in the shower. Dozing."

"Sorry, but I figured you'd want to know about that stock. Shawn called me a few minutes ago. He checked it out this afternoon, but just got around to calling now."

"Good."

"But I don't suppose the information has any value now. Since Squires has got his killer."

"Wrong."

"It's really privileged information, you know."

"Then I assume the privilege of knowing. Don't tease, Ed. I'm too tired to be teased."

Which was as bold a lie as I had told in a long time. I felt renewed and ready—come what may.

"Okay. Turns out that the company is capitalized for 1,000 shares of capital stock, 900 of which is issued to Wilfred J. Tattersby, 100 to Nancy Ann Garfinkel. Tattersby is president and treasurer. Garfinkel is vice president and secretary. Date of incorporation, August 1984. Also authorized to be issued are 10,000 shares of redeemable preference stock, terms of which are to be determined by the company's board of trustees at the time of issuance. Purpose of the company is investment management. That's about it."

"What about the company address?"

"Oh yes. 3254 Greenfield Road, Royal Oak. Conquistador Apartments. Apartment 203."

"I know those apartments. Dotty Dorrance used to live there. Neat little one- and two-room units. Queer place for a business address. It's strictly residential, I'm sure."

"Initial addresses aren't necessarily permanent addresses. Likely this is the address of the company secretary at the time of incorporation. Nancy Garfinkel. Probably the company has a different address now, since it's presumably in full operation. Hold on a minute."

I knew he must be riffling through the telephone directory, so there was no point in my doing it, too.

"Not listed," he said. "Neither the old address nor any new one."

"Strange," I said.

"Not necessarily."

Lawyers always have credible alternatives to any situation, I've noticed.

"Probably they're pretty much a closed corporation dealing with just a few people. Major investor's got to be Tattersby himself, so he's probably incorporated his resources to save on personal taxes. Works with a few friends only. No need to advertise because he's not after new investors."

"So where does that leave us?"

"You—not us. Where you ought to be. Out of their business, which isn't any of yours."

"Is that your professional advice, Counselor?"

"It is."

"Fine. Case closed. Send me your bill and it will be paid at my earliest convenience."

"Janie—thank God it worked out this way. You could have been in the kind of trouble nobody could have gotten you out of!"

I hate being called Janie and Ed is the only person I let get away with it sometimes because, despite my protests, there's something in his paternal nature that evokes the diminutive toward me in times of stress and high emotion.

"Well, it's nice to know you would have tried to get me out even if you couldn't have, Eddie," I said. "And thanks for the information. Good night."

I hung up, but I hadn't moved five steps from the phone before it was ringing back at me. In response to my hello, a pseudo-irate voice said, "Don't call me Eddie!" and the line clicked dead.

12

I thought long and hard about the situation before I fell asleep, and when I woke I lay in bed thinking some more. Two conclusions emerged from my mental meanderings. First, if Harry's murder was related to Emmett Harvey's dealings with somebody at the Colorado Beef House, I could not protect Dr. Manchester's confidentiality for long. Second, the only person who might shed some real light on the murder was at this moment locked up in the Oakland County jail. Somehow I had to have a private talk with Rick Janescu. The problem was how.

Use your ingenuity, J.D., I told myself. You're famous for round-abouting your way to the middle of mazes, so plot a deception, execute it in your inimitable style, and come up a winner as usual. Sister. Pretend to be Rick's sister and get a few family minutes with him. If he was accused of being drunk and disorderly, I might have succeeded with such a ruse, but the guardians of law and order were not likely to take the word of even so skillful a dissembler as myself with a prisoner certain to be indicted for first-degree murder. They would demand plenty of identification and would check out every claim I made before granting me a conference, and I would probably end up in jail myself.

How then? I was eating toast and marmalade before a practical plan flashed through my mind with the brilliance of a flaring meteor. Aside from close relatives, who might be permitted to talk with a prisoner charged with murder? I reached for the phone, hoping to catch Ed before he left for the Glass House, where he labored when he was not in courtrooms representing Ford Motor Company, and I was lucky.

"I apologize for being cranky with you last night," I said.

"You always make your apologies at ten to eight in the morning?" he asked suspiciously. "When people are shaving?"

"Only with those near and dear to me. I was wondering whether you'll be free for lunch. Maybe we could have a late lunch and spend the afternoon together."

"To do what?"

"Oh—things various and sundry."

"Where?"

"Here and there. Wherever."

"I mean, where do you want to have lunch? Not that overpriced beef-fish house, I hope."

"Pick a place and a time, and I'll be there, my sweet."

I heard him snapping over pages in his pocket appointment book before he said, "I'm getting tired of Moffat's, and it's always so damn crowded."

"How about the Kingsley Inn, then? It won't be crowded after one on a Tuesday."

"Good. I can pick you up at one-thirty."

The Kingsley Inn on Woodward, halfway between Birmingham and Pontiac, has always been one of the two or three premier eating places in Bloomfield Hills, the wealthiest of Detroit's suburban areas where most of the top auto executives and athlete millionaires choose to live—George Romney, Lee Iacocca, Chet Lemon, Al Kaline, Dave Bing, Gordie Howe when he was still with the Red Wings, as well as the most flourishing attorneys and medical specialists. Homes range from a cheap $200,000 in the eighth-of-an-acre developments branching out to Adams Road east of

Woodward, to several million for the hidden estates west of Woodward along Lone Pine Road and north of the Cranbrook Schools.

Years ago, no doubt, the Kingsley was indeed a kind of inn with English-style rooms lofted above the expansive and expensive restaurant. But, as one of James Joyce's Dublin ladies noted, reminiscing on her plebian past, "everything changes." So has Woodward Avenue in Bloomfield Hills. Where once were only forested fields now sprout medical clinics, advertising agency buildings, lawyers' offices, real-estate development centers. A dozen or so years ago the Kingsley's owners decided that the time had come to expand into a modern motel-hotel complete with game rooms and swimming pools. But the elegant old restaurant they changed in only one respect: they lowered the prices to accommodate their wider and more casual clientele without destroying the quality of the food, which is not haute cuisine but "damn good eating," as Ahmad says.

It was a quarter to two when Ed parked his gray Ciera in the rear as if we were motel guests, and we went in the back way to avoid the car porters in front. "Damned if I'll pay those kids a buck to move my car twenty yards, squeal my tires and rev my engine," Ed said. "I like to dent my own doors and ding my own fenders."

"If everyone thought like you, those poor lads would never be able to work their way through college," I said, and he snorted.

We had our choice of tables, and chose a corner booth far from the bar. Ed ordered a Dewar's and water, and I ordered a Piesporter wine.

"No Margarita?" Ed asked suspiciously.

"It isn't even two o'clock," I said.

"You're not going back to the broker's office, are you?"

"No."

"But you're not done working for the day. That it?"

"Whatever do you mean, Eddie dear?"

He sulked for a good minute or more, pretending to study his menu, and I let him, pretending to study mine.

I ordered shrimp Creole and he ordered tenderloin tips on spinach noodles with a marinara sauce.

"You know, Jane, sometimes I think I should bill you for services rendered."

"Ed! You're quite competent as a stud, but really! I don't think you're good enough to make sexual prowess a source of income."

"You use me, Jane," he said, quite seriously. "I don't like to be used."

"You can bill me if that would make you feel better. How much do I owe you for last year's income tax?"

"I'm not talking about that and you know it. I'm talking about getting in touch with Shawn about Michigan Assets Corporation."

"Southeastern Michigan Assets Company."

"And about what sneaky thing it is you have in mind for me to do now, or tomorrow, or whenever."

"It isn't exactly sneaky," I said.

"Ah-ha! But that's what this lunch is all about, isn't it?"

"Is there a new law that forbids mixing business and pleasure?"

"Get to the point."

"I want to talk to Rick Janescu."

"Guy who killed your friend Harry?"

"Yes."

"What the hell for? They've got him dead to rights."

"Just the same, I'd like to talk to him. To clear up my mind about a couple of things."

"And what do you expect him to say to you? 'Yes, I did it and I'm glad.' The man's standing mute, but that doesn't mean he's going to plead guilty. Hell, no! When he gets an attorney, he'll plead innocent. Believe me."

"I do, I do. That's why I want you to go see him, to offer to defend him, maybe."

At this point, fortunately, our food arrived, and by the time the waitress had distributed it, Ed's face was not quite as red as when I had given him my proposition. He was verging on articulateness again.

"I—you—crazy! You're too much! In the first place, I'm not a criminal lawyer. I never was and never wanted to be. In the second place, the guy's guilty and I wouldn't defend him if I *was* in criminal law."

"In the third place, your food is going to get cold if you keep on first, second, and thirding me," I interrupted. "My Creole's excellent."

He attacked his beef tips and ate in silence for a time, during which I spooned two tablespoons of my Creole onto a bread dish and slid it alongside his salad.

"Try this, you'll like it," I mimed a television commercial.

Eventually he tasted it, nodded, and ate the whole morsel.

"Want to try mine?" he asked.

I dipped my coffee spoon into his beef noodles, wriggled a tip of meat into it, and lifted the load to my lips without dripping the sauce. This peace ritual completed, I resumed my attack more confidently.

"I know it sounds crazy," I began, "but I wouldn't ask you to do this if I didn't have good reasons. I told you that Janescu was one of B.T. Hickory's bodyguards, didn't I?"

"You did. And now you're going to tell me that B.T. Hickory, whoever he is, is the evil genius behind Harry's murder."

118

"That's very possible. Listen to this. On Saturday night, the night *after* Harry's body was found, Hickory offered Ahmad a job as his bodyguard."

"How in hell did Ahmad get into this? Don't tell me, I know. You trapped him, just as you're trying to trap me. Right?"

"No such thing. Realizing that I was in a quandary, he volunteered to help me, like the true gentleman that he is. But the point I'm making is that Hickory hired Ahmad to replace Janescu after Harry's body had been found."

"So what? He didn't like Janescu's work and fired him. Natural to hire somebody to take his place. What evidence do you have that there's any connection between the murder and Ahmad's hiring?"

"Remarkable coincidences ought to be established as coincidences before they are accepted as such," I stated in my most juristic manner. "We don't know that Janescu was fired. That's one thing we can determine by talking to him. And if he wasn't fired, then I'd say we have something evidential to go on. Don't you agree?"

"We'd have a reasonable suspicion, but no evidence. A man can fire an employee, especially one who doesn't have any kind of contract, at any time on any or no provocation. Defense rests."

"Uh-huh. Janescu's in Oakland County jail. Just four miles up the road."

"Where he will remain until he's formally indicted, tried, and sentenced," Ed decreed.

"What harm can it do to talk to him?"

"What good can it do? Jane, by now he's already hired a lawyer, or if he can't afford one, he'll be assigned one by the court. I can't offer to represent him just so that I can talk to him, then back out later. How would that look to my colleagues? And if this guy pinned his hopes on me, think what a trauma it would be to him when I didn't go through with my offer."

"I doubt that Janescu suffers much from trauma at this stage of his life. His eyes and ears are used to trauma. Look, you don't have to offer to represent him. You merely say that you'd like to talk to him to determine whether your conscience will let you represent him. You're here at the request of a friend who chooses to remain anonymous. That can't be such an unusual routine in a situation of this kind. Janescu must have some friends."

Ed hesitated in his response, and I knew that he had lost once again to my incomparable sophistry, which is not to say that a little Scotch, a good meal, and the nearness of me didn't help.

We drove north on Woodward until it becomes Wide Track, hung a left onto Huron, and with the glint of the Silverdome behind us, worked our way the two miles through town to Telegraph Road. The Oakland County Service Drive branches off Telegraph and leads past green pastures to the courthouse and the sheriff's headquarters, a large part of which is the jail. It is a squat, brown brick box of a building. The brick is a veneer shell, inside of which air-conditioned offices enjoy all the amenities of any modern office building, but the core of the structure is solid cement and, though modern enough architecturally, no prisoner would vouch for its amenities.

The desk sergeant was bored and seemed to enjoy the distraction of our company. He examined Ed's credentials, made a phone call, then another, and finally summoned a junior officer, who escorted us to an interview room.

"You can wait in here," he said.

"In here" turned out to be a windowless, one-doored conference room furnished with a six-foot-long, three-foot-wide drawerless table, and four oak armchairs. This is no place to get trapped in a fire, I thought, staring at the high-gloss beige walls as featureless as a stretch of level desert. The silence grew heavy as we waited. There was life outside, we knew, because occasionally a chirrup of activity penetrated the solid closed door, but there was no definition to the sounds and we felt divorced from the endeavors they represented.

"I hope he won't be long in coming," I said to break the silence, and was shocked that my voice bounced off the walls.

"We can still get out of this," Ed said, almost in a whisper. "All we have to do is walk out."

Finally—it may have been all of eight minutes—the door opened and Janescu, his hands cuffed in front of him, came in along with two police officers. One of them escorted him to the table and pulled a chair out from it so he could sit facing us.

"We'll be right outside the door," he said. "He gives you any trouble, just holler."

He and his colleague left the room, but the door remained open just a crack.

Janescu was wearing a light gray, one-piece cotton suit that buttoned up the front like a child's winter pajamas, or a chic lady's fashionable jumpsuit. But this was no jumpsuit—it was jail garb which could be changed daily or weekly for another that looked just like it and like the one that would be issued the next day or next week. It was a hygienic perk reserved for the long-term residents of the jail awaiting trial in six or eight or twenty-three weeks, depending on the docket calendar of the court.

Janescu himself, perhaps because of the almost colorless suit, looked much larger than I remembered him from the Colorado Beef House. Of course, there he had been sitting alongside buffalo-big Buford. His hair, naturally curly, needed no combing, and he was clean shaven beneath his twisted nose, which must have been broken several times. At close range the scar tissue about his eyebrows, what there was left of them, was whiter than the rest of his face. His eyes, as much gray as blue, seemed to me more hurt than angry as he looked across the table at us.

"Took you long enough to get here," he said.

I was not surprised that his voice was a gravelly tenor.

"I'm Edward Rogers," Ed said. "I'm an attorney. And this is . . ."

"I'm his associate," I interrupted.

"Nice to meetcha," Janescu responded, and I felt his eyes assessing what he could see of my figure. "Mr. Hickory sent you to arrange my bail?"

The question was directed as much to me as to Ed, which I took as a compliment.

"No," Ed replied. "You're being held without bail. That's usual in charges of first-degree murder, though you haven't been formally indicted yet."

"You mean I got to stay here till I'm tried?"

"I'm afraid so, Mr. Janescu. Your indictment, I'm afraid, is a foregone conclusion. I want you to understand, however, that Mr. Hickory did not send me."

Janescu seemed puzzled for a moment, but only for a moment.

"Okay, okay, he dint send you. What's the game?"

Ed had no idea how to answer this question, so I took over.

"Mr. Janescu, Mr. Rogers is telling you the truth when he says that Mr. Hickory did not send him to represent you. Mr. Hickory, I assume, is a friend to whom you have appealed for help."

The gray-blue eyes squinted at me for ten seconds, then at Ed, and back at me.

"Let's just say a friend who wishes to remain unknown for now sent us," I said. "But not Mr. Hickory."

"Couldn't be Tim Leary. He hates my guts!"

"Not Mr. Leary either," I said. "Now, before we can determine whether we can represent you, we have to have some idea of what really happened. Will you answer our questions as honestly as you can?"

"Jee-sus! I don't know what's going down, honest I don't!"

"Perhaps together, we can make some sense of it. First of all, did you kill Harry Jenkins?"

"Christ no! I dint hardly know the guy. Met him once or twice at Hazel Park when they still ran the thoroughbreds there, then I never seen him again till week before last when he came in a restaurant I was at."

"What restaurant was that?"

"Colorado Beef House. It's just off Fifteen Mile Road past John R. He recognized me and bought me a drink."

"But you did not kill him?"

"No way, miss, honest to God!"

"You drove him home, did you? Or to another bar perhaps?"

"No I dint. He come back to this Beef House the next day, see, and right along all last week. I guess he was bettin' with a bookie near there 'cause he always had the form with him, y'know? But I hardly ever talked to him 'cept to say hello."

"But the police found your lighter in Jenkins's pocket, and a tear from Jenkins's trousers in the trunk of your car. How do you explain that?"

"They gotta be lyin'!"

"No, they're not, Rick—may I call you Rick?"

"Sure."

"I've seen the lighter and I checked with the coroner, Dr. Costos, who's a friend of mine, and he confirms that there was a tear in Jenkins's trousers," I lied. "I don't know about the hairs in your trunk, but I hardly think the police would say they were there if they weren't."

Janescu sat staring down at the table for a time, his big-knuckled hands squeezed tightly together. I couldn't tell whether he was sulking or trying to think.

"Jee-sus, I don't know!" he muttered, then looked up at me. "You telling me the truth. Hickory dint send you?"

"I assure you, Rick, we have never talked with this Mr. Hickory. Is he involved in this affair? Is that it?"

Suddenly, Janescu snapped from his slump to a posture of sitting attention, and slammed his fists onto the tabletop.

"Hey!" he said. "You're cops! You're tryin' to trick me!"

"Jane, I told you this was a foolish idea," Ed said. "Let's get out of here."

"Not yet," I said. "Give him one of your professional cards, Ed. Please."

Reluctantly, Ed slipped a card from his wallet, identifying him as an attorney-at-law, of counsel to the Ford Motor Company, and handed it to Janescu.

"This don't mean a thing," he said. "Anybody can get cards printed."

"I suppose so," I said. "But evidence obtained by such a deception as you imagine we are trying to perpetrate on you would never be permitted in a court of law. I assure you, Rick, we are not police. And we are trying to help you."

"Oh, yeah? Why?"

It was a fair question and, I decided, deserving of an honest answer.

"Very well, I'll tell you why we're here, Rick. Harry Jenkins's wife has long been a dear friend of mine. Milly can't understand why you would want to kill her husband. Harry was an easy-come, easy-go guy who wouldn't hurt a soul. She never heard of you, and—

well—I told her I'd talk to you. She's a very religious person, and she doesn't want anyone to suffer unjustly. If you didn't actually kill her husband, she doesn't want you to go to jail for it."

I assumed my honest-Jane, how-could-I-tell-a-lie look and hoped that Ed wouldn't give me away with a laugh or some ejaculation of indignation. Actually, I believe he was too astounded to register any emotion verbally.

Finally, Janescu said, tentatively, "I dint do it, miss. Swear to God, I dint!"

I closed my eyes and nodded several times.

"We want to believe you, Rick. And we want to help you. But you've got to help us. Tell us what happened, how you got involved."

"I just work for Mr. Hickory. I do what he tells me to."

"What did he tell you to do, Rick?"

"Friday night. About nine-thirty, I think. He tole me there'd been a accident, that a guy got drunk and fell down in the parking lot and broke his neck. Said it wouldn't be good for the restaurant if he was found on the property. Insurance wasn't up to date or something, and tole me and Tim to drive him a couple of miles away and dump him where nobody would find him till tomorrow. Tole me to load him in the trunk of my car and get him out of there."

"Where was the body?"

"In the basement. I backed my car up to the loading stairs, and Tim and me carried him up and put him in the trunk. That's all I did, miss, honest!"

"And you took him to Acacia Cemetery?"

"We dint know where to take him, but since Mr. Hickory tole us not to come back to the restaurant, and Tim lives in Berkley, he said maybe that would be a good place to dump him 'cause nobody goes in cemeteries at night, and it was kind of on our way to Tim's place. So we turned the lights out and swung in the graveyard and there was this grave already dug. I know what I did was wrong but I was trying to help the restaurant, y'know. And the man was dead. Nothing I could do to help him."

"Does Mr. Hickory own part of the restaurant, Rick?"

"Terry owns it. Terry's a good friend of his. I guess he was doing it to help Terry."

"Don't the police believe your story?"

"I dint tell them nothing! I'm waitin' for my lawyers. You guys."

Peering across the table at me, his curly head emerging low from his huge shoulders with his near browless eyes concentrated on mine, he reminded me of a faithful but dumb Saint Bernard dog.

"God must like you, Rick," I said. "If we hadn't decided to look in on you, you'd be waiting for your lawyers until the day you got into court."

"Mr. Hickory will send somebody, if he dint send you."

"Really? Do you really believe that, Rick? How come your friend Tim isn't in jail? He's as guilty as you after the fact."

"It was my car, I guess."

"And your lighter. How do you suppose your lighter got into Harry Jenkins's pocket?"

"I swear I don't know, miss. I been thinkin' 'bout that though. I remember Tim asked me for a light while we was waitin' for the green to turn onto Southfield off Fourteen Mile, and I gave him my lighter. I remember that. Maybe he dropped it when we were haulin' the body out of the trunk."

"And it dropped into Harry Jenkins's coat pocket? Really, Rick!"

"Yeah. I guess not. You telling me he put it there deliberate, ain't you?"

"You've already considered that possibility, haven't you?"

"I thought about it."

"Did you and Tim get along all right?"

"He did his job, I did mine."

"What was his job exactly?"

"He was Mr. Hickory's gun."

"And yours?"

"I was his muscle. You know, I kept the jerks and drunks away from him. Anybody who had a yen to knock him. After a few drinks, he'd get pretty mouthy, y'know? Tim—he watched out for guys who might want to bump him for good."

"Why would Tim plant that lighter of yours on Harry's body, Rick? Did he hate you that much?"

"Naw, naw. We got along. Didn't like him, he didn't like me, but it was our jobs. We got along."

"Then why? There can only be one reason, and I think you're bright enough to figure it out, even though you don't want to admit it."

The head sank toward the tabletop and I lost sight of the Saint Bernard eyes. It began to bob up and down slowly.

"Yeah. Mr. Hickory musta tole him to," he said.

Suddenly, his fists and cuffs rose up and then crashed down on the tabletop.

"Why!" he demanded. "Why, fer God's sake! I did my job good!"

The door swung inward and a guard stepped into the room, glanced at us, then retreated outside.

"There can be only one reason, Rick. Harry Jenkins didn't fall down and break his neck. He was murdered, and whoever did it needed a fall guy to take the blame for it. You were elected."

This was not exactly news to Janescu, but hearing someone other than himself utter it aloud visibly shocked him.

"Uh-huh."

I had nothing else to ask at the moment, so I glanced at Ed, who had sat quiet as an obedient miniature poodle all during my interrogation, and nodded.

"Rick," he said, "you've been framed—that's perfectly clear. But hang tough a while, and we'll see what we can do. Another lawyer will come and talk to you, take down your statement in a day or so. Cooperate with him as you have with us, and there's a good chance that we can get you free of the charges against you. However, moving that body was in itself a serious felony and you'll have to pay for that. Okay?"

Ed stood up, and held his hand across the table.

"Okay," Janescu said, standing and shaking Ed's hand awkwardly with his fingertips.

"I'll get the guards," Ed said, and moved toward the door.

"Thanks, miss," Janescu said to me. "I dint get your name."

"Mulroy."

"Well, thanks."

The guards were now on each side of him, walking him toward the door, where he paused and turned back to us.

"You thank Harry's wife for me, Miss Mulloy," he called back. "Tell her I never touched Harry when he was alive, and I'm sorry for what happened."

Then he was gone.

13

It was four-thirty when we swung out of the municipal complex onto Telegraph Road and headed south toward Birmingham and cocktails at Moffat's. The first ripples of what would soon be the daily let-me-get-to-my-home-in-the-suburbs wave were already evident, but we were going the other way and traffic was ordinary.

"Let's take Lone Pine over to Woodward," I suggested.

"Get out of the flow. Good," Ed agreed.

We did the loop at Lone Pine, passed the Bloomfield Hills library, and started down the two-lane, two-way traffic asphalt at twenty-five miles an hour toward the Cranbrook schools. This two-mile drive runs between rows of acre-size lots on which are built some of the most elegant customized homes in the country. The most prestigious cannot be seen at all, being shielded from view by tree-high shrubs as dense as privet hedges. It is a stretch of road one can relax and think on.

"Leonard," Ed said. "I'll ask Leonard Shell to defend him."

"Do I know him?"

"You met him two years ago at the Dearborn Hyatt. The Michigan Bar Association convention."

"I met half a hundred lawyers at that cocktail party. Which one was he?"

"Ordinary-looking kind of guy. About five-nine, brown hair, wears horn-rimmed glasses."

"Oh, him?"

"Don't be cute. He's one of the best in the state, though he usually stays out of the headlines. He lets one of his juniors do the talking in court, but he does the research, sets up the case, directs the questions."

"And he's very cheap, of course."

"If the client has a lot of money, he charges a lot of money. Leonard's father was a shrewd market investor, and he left Leonard tens of thousands of shares of Digital Equipment, National Medical Enterprises, and Ball Corporation stock which he bought before they made their big moves."

"You're a confidant of Leonard, are you?"

"I'm his tax man, baby. Leonard takes in more than a million a year in dividends alone. He can afford to select only those cases that he believes in, whether there's a decent fee in them or not."

Most of Ed's work is performed in the interests of the Ford Motor Company, from which he draws a full-time salary, but he has his own clients, too, and not all of them renege on cash payments, like me. I think the reason he drives a GM car, rather than a Ford product (which he could buy at a substantial discount), is that he likes to think of himself as his own man, and except when he's with me, he is.

"So you agree with me, then, that Janescu was set up?"

"Unless he's the most skillful liar I ever met, even more skillful than you—which I doubt is possible in this world—yes."

"I blush with pride!"

"He's got nothing going right now. I think he'll be interested."

"Do you want me to talk to him?"

"Negative!"

"He'll want to know what Harry was doing, won't he?"

"Maybe, maybe not. We still aren't sure that your investigation had anything to do with the killing. I'll tell him that Harry must have been working on a case and let it go at that for now. That way, your client and Harvey will be protected, at least for a while."

We had crossed Lasher Road and were now gliding by the old red brick wall that hides the Cranbrook school grounds from public view. As we paused at the crossing before the gated entrance to the school and gardens, I said, "Is Leonard married, Ed?"

"No."

We moved ahead down the slope toward the splendid gothic anomaly that is Christ Church Cranbrook. Ed noticed the smile on my lips.

"Why do you ask that?"

"I was just thinking. A man who's very wealthy, intelligent, of high moral standard—he'd be quite a catch for a girl who takes an interest in righting wrongs, wouldn't he?"

"You know a girl like that, I'll be glad to introduce her to him," Ed replied, and I dropped the subject. It doesn't hurt to scratch the skin of a man's ego, but it's a foolish woman who deliberately pierces it.

We loitered at Moffat's for the remainder of the afternoon, and dallied at my place most of the evening. But no matter what my body may have been doing, my sentient brain was feeling its way out of the fog that misted its view. And by the time I was ready to get into bed for the second time in a few hours, this time alone, I knew what had to be done and done quickly: I had to confront Emmett Harvey and try to find out what had happened when he went into the kitchen, or beyond it, last Friday night. Was it possible that Emmett was involved in Harry's murder? I could not bring myself to believe this, and yet, crime history is full of examples of schizoid killers whose double lives, until the moment of revelation, never contradicted each other.

Having decided what had to be done, the next morning over coffee and toast I worried about the tactics of how to do it. I considered first the direct, upfront approach. March right into Harvey's office and take charge. Okay, buddy, the jig's up. We know (we being the authorities behind the phony badge or other credentials I would flash) you're in on the scam at the Colorado Beef House and we're giving you this one chance to come clean and maybe get out of it whole. Now talk or take the consequences!

It was a grand TV scenario, but didn't register real to me. Harvey was a methodical man who believed in order, if not in law; he would resent my having deceived him; he did not seem subject to panic, as his continuing operation of his business despite his troubles indicated; and I was certain that he would examine my credentials and check on their authenticity before he even considered whether to cooperate or not. Having unmasked me, he would then banish me from his office and his sight, and my chances of further "research" there would be kaput.

So, when the direct approach isn't practical, one relies on the indirect: "By indirection find direction out." By the time I got to the office, I had my plan, but Harvey did not come in that morning, and when I asked Melissa if he was ill, she said that he had flown to Chicago to attend a seminar on the float of some new big bond issue. He would be back in the office Tuesday. Tomorrow, tomorrow, and tomorrow—time would have to creep on another twenty-four hours before I could get into action, but patience is part of the trade.

I got home at a little after three, and by five I had received two phone calls. The first was from Dr. Mansfield, and she wanted to know whether I was making any progress, a reasonable request since she was paying me nearly two hundred dollars a day and I had been on the job for nearly two full weeks.

"Yes, I'm learning a good bit," I told her. "But unfortunately I can't reveal what I've discovered just yet because I'm not sure how much of it concerns your brother-in-law."

"Then he is in trouble?"

"I'm sure of that, yes. But another woman isn't the problem. I know that."

"That's some consolation. Have you told Charlotte?"

"I've talked with her but I'd prefer that you don't press her."

"Yes, of course. Shall I send you some money?"

"Not until I've finished. Some of what I'm doing, perhaps, oughtn't to be charged to you. I hope you can be patient a little longer, Doctor."

The second call was from Ed.

"Two things," he said, all business after Sunday's sensual dalliance. "First, I've talked to Leonard and he's interested. Wouldn't say whether he'll take the case until he talks with Janescu himself, but I think he will."

"Good."

"Second, I went to see Jim Squires and got a copy of the coroner's report. Leonard will need it and is entitled to it. Cause of death was a broken neck inflicted by a severe blow with a rusty iron bar, evidenced by particles in the area of contact. There's a funny item in the report. 'Crystallization in certain capillaries and other organs suggests that the body may have been under severe refrigeration for a time after death.' "

"Wow!"

"Wow what?"

"Could he tell how long Harry had been dead before he was found?"

"That's the problem. The refrigeration makes it difficult to be certain. He guesses that he was refrigerated shortly after death. And that he was exposed to the cool night air for several hours before he was discovered. But he can't be very specific."

"Well, at least we know now where Harry spent Friday night and most of Saturday."

"How, not where."

"I'm betting on both," I said. "You're a darling to call and I don't know how I'd ever get along without you."

"Probably very well," Ed said. "You want I should sing like Sinatra?"

I wondered how Ahmad was making out on his new job, but had no intention of getting up at three or four in the morning to call him (and I had better sense than to call him when I got up at a little past seven). He would call me when there was anything to report.

At the office, the next day, my chance came just before noon, after Melissa had left for lunch. Harvey had spent the morning in his office, but now he came out to give Essie some typing, and I happened to be on my way out for lunch when he turned from the receptionist's desk and almost knocked me over.

"Sorry," he mumbled. "Didn't see you there."

"It was my fault. I'm sorry."

He started around me and had almost made it when I said, "Oh, Mr. Harvey—can I talk to you for a minute?"

At first I thought he was going to refuse, but then, apparently recognizing me and recalling the fortuitous way I had come to be here, he nodded his assent and led the way into his office, taking care not to close the door.

"Had enough, have you?" he asked, sitting down at his desk.

134

"Enough?" I echoed, also sitting down alongside his desk.

"Working here," he explained. "Found out it's not your bag?"

"Oh, no. I like it very much. I'm truly enjoying it. Melissa is such a good teacher!"

"She knows the business certainly, backward and forward—no doubt about that."

There was an awkward pause.

"What was it you wanted to see me about?" he asked.

"Oh, yes! I should have mentioned it before, I intended to, but then you were out of town yesterday and it just slipped my mind till we almost bumped heads. Let me see, last Friday I guess it was, a man called and asked for the price of a stock—Michigan Eastern—no, Southeastern Michigan Assets Company, that was it. I checked for it on the computer but there was no entry, then I went through our files and couldn't find it either. It isn't listed on any of the markets in the *Journal* and it isn't in Standard & Poor's stock guide, so I asked the man if I could call him back but he said he'd call us back. I asked Melissa about it later and she doesn't know anything about the stock. I thought I ought to mention it to you, that's all."

"I see. The caller didn't leave his name?"

"No. He just said that he understood we handled the stock and he wanted a price on it."

"To sell or to buy?"

"He didn't say, and I didn't think to ask him. I should have, shouldn't I? There's usually a difference when it's over the counter, isn't there?"

"That's all he said?"

"Yes. I got the impression, though, that he was calling from a public place. There was a lot of laughter and voices in the background, you know, and I heard a woman's voice very distinctly say, 'Two jaybees and a beam, Joe,' whatever that means."

"Yes. Well, thanks for mentioning it."

I rose and started toward the door, then turned back.

"If he calls again, shall I tell him we don't handle that stock, Mr. Harvey?"

"No, don't do that. We can handle any stock. Put him through to me. If I'm not here, get his phone number and tell him that I'll call him back as soon as I get in."

"Yes, sir."

So what did you accomplish with that neatly contrived tête-à-tête, J. D., I asked myself as I sat in a sunny corner of Wendy's nibbling on my self-made salad. The sky was bright blue, the sun streamed down, but the wind-driven air was cold enough to rosy cheeks and chap lips. Nobody would ever write a sonnet celebrating November in Michigan. It was too early to determine whether I had accomplished anything or not. My idea had been to gauge Harvey's reaction to my innocent inquiries. His reactions had been calm and collected and would have aroused no suspicion in the mind of any objective observer. But his final directive seemed significant because it authorized me to direct any repeat call only to him: not to Tony, or Al, or Melissa, or anyone except him. So congratulations on a great bit of detection, J. D.; you've discovered what you already knew to be true—that old Emmett is handling the SMACO account all by his lonesome. I decided I might as well get in the acronymic spirit of modern journalism and the U.S. government.

On the other hand (the optimistic one, if hands have moods), few fishermen ever catch fish without bait. If strangers were getting interested in such a privately held stock, somebody must be talking about it, somebody who owns it or knows and envies somebody who owns it. Was this good for Harvey in his dealings with Terence Garfinkel and his wife, not to mention Wilfred

Tattersby, president of SMACO? Who the hell was Wilfred Tattersby, anyway? I'd checked him in the phone directories but he wasn't listed. How do you locate a man about whose whereabouts you haven't a clue? Was he always on the road, as Harvey's SMACO file reported? Harry had been great at the leg game, but he had traced his last "residence unknown' assignment.

One thing I needed was a replacement for Harry, I decided as I wheeled out of the parking lot and headed back to the office. I had used Elsa Bailey a couple of times in the past, but never in a case that looked dangerous. Elsa was a whiz at getting information from chatty women or males on the make, she was fine in locating runaway wives, husbands, or teenagers. But to expose her to people to whom killing seemed a routine solution to a problem was unthinkable. The truth was that, had I known the kind of people I would be dealing with, I would never have asked Harry to help me. Harry didn't even carry a gun. Conclusion: The only replacement for Harry I would feel guiltless to rely on was myself.

I turned in the office driveway, swung around the rear to the parking lot, and was about to turn off my engine when I looked up and saw Harvey walking toward his Oldsmobile 98 parked in its usual reserved space in row one. Under his arm was a brown manila envelope large enough to hold a filing folder. Had our conversation stirred some stumps? I wondered and watched, then as he pulled out and headed for 16 Mile Road, I backed out of my parking slot and followed.

Why should I work if the boss wasn't going to?

14

We were moving east along Big Beaver (16 Mile) Road, as I had expected. The newly washed blue Olds three cars ahead of me was easy to follow. Traffic wasn't heavy in the middle of the afternoon and no one was moving much faster than the forty-mile speed limit. At Livernois, two cars and a tan panel truck darted in front of me making rights when traffic had cleared, but the panel truck turned off a few buildings down the road so that I could from time to time glimpse the blue Olds five cars up the line. It didn't really matter if I lost sight of it altogether; I was pretty sure where it was going, and I was right: it swung south on John R, then east on Maple, and finally turned into the parking lot of the Colorado Beef House.

I drove past the restaurant to the next left loop, moved back west, and drove into the mall parking lot across the road anchored by a K-Mart and a Farmer Jack supermarket.

I found a parking space against the rail, switched off the engine, and sat staring across the busy road to the entrance of the Beef House. Watching and waiting are not my favorite pastimes, especially when I am totally unprepared without paperback, newspaper, or cross-word puzzle. I thought of reading the operator's manual that had come with my car a year ago and was still snugly tucked in the bottom of my glove compartment, but I rejected this idea. Suppose I got so engrossed in the stylish descriptions, complete with illustrations and diagrams, that I forgot my assignment? I couldn't risk it. Besides, I knew how to operate this beautiful beige beauty and if I was doing something wrong, I didn't want to know about it.

More people were coming out of the Beef House now than were going in—about a five to one ratio, which was to be expected since it was past two o'clock and too early for the cocktail crowd. I rolled down my window an inch or two and let in a stream of thirty-degree air. For a time it was refreshing, then just plain cold as it twisted into my hair, and I had to roll the window closed.

Twenty minutes passed, then thirty. I had just decided to get out of the car and walk a little when the Beef House door opened and Harvey and Terry Garfinkel came out together. Terry wore no topcoat, and he stood with his hands in his pockets while he talked, saying something, I suppose, that he had forgotten to say inside, or that he found inappropriate to say inside. Harvey still carried the brown manila envelope, and I made a mental note to return to the office after hours and have a look at it. Terry ducked back into the building, and Harvey went down the sidewalk into the parking lot to get his car. I waited until he pulled out and headed west back toward the office before I decided that Margarita time had just about arrived. I locked my car, crossed the road, and entered the Beef House for the third time in my life.

Nanette was nowhere visible, so I decided to sit at the bar, which was perhaps a third occupied. I chose a seat next to the serving well—one often learns things of interest about a place from the chatter of waitresses at bar wells—and waited for the bartendress, a Marilyn Monroe type but taller, stronger, more athletically contoured despite her forty-inch bustline, to notice me. She was talking to a man and his girlfriend at the bar's bend, interspersing her narration with raised hand gestures and head noddings to emphasize her words. When she finally finished, both the man and the woman laughed heartily, if not sincerely. She confronted me then, slapping a four-by-four paper doily in front of me.

"You alone, honey?" she asked in a very un-Marilyn-like alto voice.

"Right now, yes."

"I gotcha. What're ya gonna have?"

"Maragarita up. Very little salt on the rim."

She knew her business. Expertly, she aerated and measured the tequila as she poured it into the mixing glass, raising the bottle about sixteen inches above the glass with the liquor spouting out, then lowering it to glass edge. She twirled my frosted glass tenderly in the salt saucer, set it in front of me, and when she poured the finished product, it was exactly the right amount to fill in my glass to the rim.

"What's it doin' out?" she asked. "Any snow yet?"

"No. Windy but no snow."

She rang up my tab, but before she could set it down in front of me, a familiar voice said over my shoulder, "That's mine, Lorelei." I turned to find Nathan standing behind me. He sat down at my side, and unasked, Lorelei poured him a cup of decaf.

"I cannot believe that you have returned with a complaint about our earrings," Nathan said.

"Oh, no. They're lovely!"

"May I hope, then, that you may be contemplating some other purchase?"

"Well, I just stopped in because I was in the neighborhood on some business and it's too late to go back to the office now. But since you're here, yes, I am thinking of buying another piece from you. That necklace—have you sold it yet to Mr. What's-His-Name? The big man?"

"Mr. Hickory?"

"Yes."

"I haven't showed it to him lately. It's a bit early for my Christmas trade, Miss Mulroy. However, if you are interested, I shall set it aside for you until you can examine it again, evaluate it. Unfortunately, I do not have my case with me or I should let you take it with you now. Perhaps you would like to have lunch with me tomorrow, or Friday?"

"Well, I don't want to steal it from Mr. Hickory. Maybe you can ask him whether he's seriously interested in purchasing it. If he isn't, then we can talk."

During our conversation, Lorelei had been emptying glasses from the automatic dishwasher just to Nathan's left. She had been listening and made no pretence of hiding her interest.

"Nathan!" she said. "You damn well better ask B. T. before you sell that necklace because *I* want it!"

Nathan stared at her sternly, a frown on his face.

"Well, I *do* want it!" Lorelei said, then wilting under Nathan's disapproval, she walked slowly to her friends at the bar bend.

Nathan shook his head sadly.

"So many young people today," he said, "have no sense of propriety. No concept of courtesy. Some journalist or other has called them the 'gimme generation.' An apt characterization."

He then looked directly into my eyes.

"A generalization, of course. There are exceptions, as you yourself demonstrate. I am tempted now not to sell Mr. Hickory the Lanzetti necklace under any circumstances."

"You mustn't punish him because of her," I said. "I wouldn't want the necklace under those circumstances. It's a very lovely thing. I understand how Lorelei feels. Is she related to Mr. Hickory?"

Nathan chuckled.

"That is probably the precise word, Miss Mulroy. There is a definite relationship between them, yes."

From the corner of my eye I saw Terry Garfinkel emerge into view and survey the bar.

"I see," I said, as Terry approached us.

"I'm ready to go," he said to Nathan.

Nathan nodded.

"Forgive me but I must leave. A funeral—an unavoidable duty. But I shall be here Friday about noon, and I'll have the necklace if you should care to see it again."

He put three dollars on my bar tab, then stood, bowed briefly, and walked off with Terry at his side, trailing him slightly, like a loyal terrier and its master. He was no sooner out of sight than Lorelei hurried back to me. She leaned across the bar intimately—not only in manner but in fact, for I could peer down her cleavage almost to her navel; it was quite a valley view.

"Look, honey," she said in a husky whisper almost as deep as her cleavage, "I hope you don't mind me hornin' in your talk with that old Jew pawnbroker, but B. T. and me, see, we have sort of an understanding, you know what I mean, and he as much as promised me that necklace. So I been countin' on it for Christmas. That's why I said what I did."

"I understand, Lorelei—is that your real name?"

"Well, kinda. It's Laura, really, but first place I worked was a club in Windsor, and the manager liked to call his girls by fancy names—so he called me Lorelei. They had tabletop bare-bosom dancing, you know, they're all over the place in Windsor now, but when he wanted to move me from the bar to dancing, I said, 'Screw you, buddy!' and quit. I ain't strippin' in public for every Tom, Dick, and John to get his jollys off— no way! Would you?"

"Never!" I said, and meant it.

" 'Course, you got a right to buy the necklace if you really want it, I know that."

"I don't think I could afford it," I said. "Nathan told me it's worth about six thousand dollars."

Lorelei was visibly stunned.

"That much?" she said finally.

"Oh yes. And I believe him. I know a good bit about gold work."

"Gee! I don't know now. I'd be scairt to wear it!"

"Well, you'd hardly wear it to work here. It's the kind of jewelry you keep in a safe deposit box, and wear only on special occasions."

"Yeah? Well, I ain't got a safe deposit box, and what good's jewelry if you can't wear it whenever you feel like it. Gotta go. Here come the four o'clocks."

Half a dozen men ready for the day's relief, obviously regulars, were checking their topcoats. Lorelei began slapping doilies in front of bar chairs and was mixing drinks before the men found seats. She seemed to know exactly what each one would order.

By now the tables were all unoccupied. A busboy who looked to be Puerto Rican was busily whipping off old tablecloths and replacing them with clean ones. More men drifted in to sit at or stand by the bar for their late afternoon pick-up libation, and I figured that if I didn't want to be mistaken for a pick-up of a different kind, I'd better absent myself, so I slipped a dollar bill under my empty glass and headed for the ladies' room. But I didn't go there directly. The washrooms were located off a brief corridor that ended in front of a door marked *Private*. Well, I was a private eye, wasn't I? I slipped through the door and found myself standing a yard in front of what any decent seaman would have called a "ladder," so steep was its angle of descent. A dim light rose from what apparently was the restaurant's storage basement. I listened for a moment, then, hearing nothing, quietly, on the soles of my Cuban-heeled shoes, descended twelve steep risers to the basement's cement floor.

The light was coming from a sixty-watt bulb hung from the center of the ceiling. I knew what I was looking for but I didn't know what it might look like. The walls were lined with white porcelain-fronted chests that I took to be refrigeration units. There were at least ten of them, small, medium, and two quite large. At the far end of the room was an aluminum-sided container. I opened one small and one medium-size freezer and found what I expected to find—bags of frozen peas, corn, peas-corn-and-carrots mix, beans, broccoli, lima beans, brussels sprouts, and so forth. I opened one of the large freezers and it was loaded with what I took to be wrapped strip steaks in packages of six. The other large freezer was fitted with a steel hinge and was padlocked. Prime steaks, I wondered, not to be confused by careless kitchen help with U.S.D.A.? I opened the wedge latch handle to the aluminum unit: a bright light switched on automatically and I found myself staring at sides of beef, lamb, and veal hanging along the walls from built-in hooks. Apparently the Colorado Beef House did its own butchering, and presumably the beef hanging here was imported from the Colorado-Kansas-Montana region. This is the age of honesty in advertising, isn't it? Next time Ed and I ate here, I would insist on his ordering a Colorado rib of beef. The cold suddenly penetrated my clothing and I closed the door with a shudder as an image of Harry's body lying on the blood-stained slats that were the floor of this meat-storage unit flashed across my mind-screen. I moved quickly toward the stairwell and almost missed what I had really come to find. Lying on a shelf beneath the stairs, along with a hammer, two screwdrivers, and a pair of pliers, was a four-foot long crowbar. It was made of iron, and was rusty!

How to get it out of the restaurant?

I couldn't very well carry it under my arm like a German general's riding crop and march out the front door past Nanette and the coat-check girl without attracting attention. I considered opening the supply doorway that led to a six-step stairway onto a spur from the parking area, the restaurant's loading dock. But the bolts to the thick door were heavy and tight, and jerking them open would screech my presence to those above who would recognize the sound.

Finally, I wrapped a Kleenex around the claw of the crooked end, hooked it sidewise in the "V" of my sweater and under the center elastic of my brassiere, belted my coat as tightly as I could, and started up the stairs, trying to control the tendency of the iron to swing by pressing my purse against my stomach. I was halfway up the stairs when the door at the top opened and I found myself staring up into the crinkled face of a little elderly man wearing black trousers and a red vest, like the old-time bartenders used to wear. He had a toilet plunger in one hand and a plastic bucket in the other.

I did what any intelligent, attractive woman would do under the circumstances: I smiled, then continued awkwardly up the steep staircase, clutching my purse urgently to my abdomen. He stepped aside as I reached the top so that I could pass into the carpeted corridor.

"Thank you," I said. "Can you direct me to the ladies' room?"

His eyes roamed up and down my figure, finally settling on my breast. I couldn't tell whether he was simply a dirty old man wishing he had gone to the basement a few minutes earlier, or whether the crowbar hook had slipped, giving me the appearance of a three-breasted woman. He raised the plunger and pointed.

"Ferst doowah, miss. You muster passt ut," he said in some kind of North English or Low Scotch accent.

"Silly of me. Thanks," I said, and walked into the empty washroom, where I used a lot of toilet tissue to pad the bar claw and adjusted my clothing as best I could in the privacy of a booth.

Nobody paid any attention to me when I left the restaurant a few minutes later.

15

When I got home a few minutes before five, I left the iron in the trunk of my Camaro, drew a tub of hot water, and lay back in its gentle warmth to soothe my crowbar-savaged breastbone, and to think.

I was as near certain as a person could be, without actually being certain, that in the trunk of my car was Harry's murder weapon. Whether the police lab technicians could actually demonstrate that the particles in the skin of Harry's neck came from this bar or not, I didn't know, but I meant to give them a chance to try. The question was, How to explain how I knew exactly where to go to find the bar without involving the Harveys? The answer was obvious, but I avoided it as long as I could, trying unsuccessfully to find some other. I would have to play the dumb dame game. "Gee, I'm sorry, Jim, but I never thought to play my phone tape for that Friday night. I only went out for a quarter of an hour that afternoon to buy some tea at Chatham's supermarket on Maple, you know, and that must have been when Harry called. I was in for the rest of the day. Actually, if I hadn't wanted to listen again to a request from a prospective client who wants me to try to find his brother for him—he called on the Thursday night before Harry was killed, I would never have caught Harry's voice at all. It's just dumb luck that I did."

And this is pretty close to what I told Jim Squires over the phone after I had dried and terry-clothed myself.

"So you went to this restaurant all by your lonesome to do a little investigating on your own, huh? You didn't want to involve the police, is that it? You were saving the taxpayers some expense money," Jim said cynically.

"I guess I should have had you send someone with me, but I wasn't sure that Harry was killed where he was calling from—all he said was that the man he was watching had come into this bar and he was making a routine report to me, that's all. For all I knew, he might have gone on to the racetrack or to some other bar or to the man's home, and it didn't seem logical to drag you into it until I had some idea of whether that was the place where Harry was actually murdered. I'm not sure of it yet. I just happened to find this crowbar in the basement of the restaurant, and it occurred to me that it might be the murder weapon. You want me to bring it over to you now?"

"I want that tape, J. D!"

"You can have a copy."

"No copy. The tape!"

"Okay, but I'm going to erase my Thursday calls."

I could hear Jim's stertorous breathing through the receiver. He really should cut out smoking that pipe, I thought.

"No use to tell you to erase nothing, is there?"

"Actually, Jim, I've already erased the Thursday calls. But I'll check again to make sure."

"Which means you will as soon as you hang up the phone. I'll have a man from forensics pick up the bar in fifteen, twenty minutes. You be there to give it to him!"

It took the man thirty-five minutes to get to my place. He slipped the bar into a long white sack, laid it in the back seat of his car, gave me an official receipt form, and left me to my meditations, which were anything but calm. I felt that I had to talk to Ahmad, to bring him up to date and find out whether he'd discovered anything that might give us a clue to the identity of the killer. If not, then it was probably time to talk turkey to Emmett Harvey. I dialed Ahmad's apartment and got no answer, then his "factory" and was informed by Deedee, his receptionist-secretary-typist-bookkeeper, that he was, as she said, "on special assignment," but would be in about ten the next morning. "Any message?"

I decided to invoke our K-Code.

"Tell him I called, Dee, and tell him it's a K-Code alert."

"K-code alert."

"That's right. He'll understand."

The K-Code alert is simply a phrase that Ahmad and I use as a message to each other that it is imperative for the receiver of the code to get in touch with the sender as soon as possible. Ahmad knows most of Detroit's professional athletes, especially those of his generation—Dave Bing, Al Kaline, Joe Schmidt, Hank Aguirre, dozens of others—and he had no trouble getting two choice box seats for the 1984 World Series behind the Tiger dugout. He had intended to take his steady, Elaine Robinson, a tall black beauty who models dresses and lingerie for Saks' special sales and for J. C. Penney's catalogues, to all three games, but she had a special assignment on the day of the second game in Detroit, so he invited me. I know that baseball is a fact of American life just like apple pie and Chevrolet Camaros, but though I like apple pie and am in love with my Camaro, I have never taken much interest in baseball. Jack Morris, I think, was pitching that day, and along about the third or fourth inning, the scoreboard began flashing a gigantic K across its entire face when certain San Diego players returned to the dugout after batting. I ignored this for a time, but finally asked what it meant.

"It's a scorecard symbol for a strikeout," Ahmad explained.

"Oh."

He borrowed the scorecard from the man sitting next to him and showed me a crossword pattern of numbers, Xs, and Ks.

"From all these squiggles and numbers and letters, a person can reconstruct what happened in every inning. Is that it?"

"You got it, babe. It's a complete code to the cognoscenti."

"I'll remember that," I said. "And the next time I'm about to strike out, I'll send you a K."

That's how our K-Code came into being, and so far in our relationship Ahmad has always responded promptly, so I knew I would hear from him in the morning. But I didn't expect it to be three-thirty A.M. In fact, when I glanced at the clockface after being jangled awake, I thought that the clock must have stopped, because nobody calls anyone except doctors or the police at three-thirty in the morning. Nobody except Ahmad in response to the K-Code.

"I didn't mean for you to call me until morning," I said, still trying to come fully awake.

"Don't yell fire if there ain't no smoke," Ahmad quoted some folksy bard or other. "You want me to call back when I wake up 'bout ten or so?"

"No, I'll be gone by then. I've dug myself into a pit and I'm not sure how to get out."

I brought him up to date on my activities, ending with my delivery of the crowbar to Jim's lab man. Ahmad was silent for a time after I had finished.

"How'd you manage to get that crowbar out of the restaurant?" he asked. "Wouldn't fit in your purse."

"It wasn't easy," I said. "I'll tell you the details sometime, but the problem *now* is, How can I jolt Harvey into telling me everything that's going down between him and Terry Garfinkel before I'm obliged to tell Jim Squires about Harvey?"

Ahmad considered some more.

"Only two ways I can think of," he said at last. "One, tell him the truth, the whole truth, and nothing but. What the hell—you working *for* him, not against him. Man can't be too hard on his woman for trying to help him."

"I've considered that. What's the other way?"

"Don't tell him the truth. Lie like a junk-bond dealer. Better than that 'cause Harvey's had experience with those. Tell him you're really from the Securities and Exchange Commission, that you've been assigned to investigate Michigan Assets Company and you want some straight answers. You know the routine."

"Southeastern Michigan Assets Company."

"That, too. Mention names. B. T. and Garfunkel, for instance."

"Garfinkel."

"Fink—funk—I'll conjugate it later. You know some of the jargon by now. Scare him into a confession after you imply that absolution for him is a possibility."

"It might work," I said. "I'll need some documents. Treasury. I should be a T-man."

"Person."

"That, too. Can you get Anse to print me what I need?"

"Will a horse eat oats? You got two hundred dollars cash?"

"Steep price for one or two bits of paper."

"Best quality paper, lady. You can keep it and use it over and over again."

"I should be so lucky! We've got to move quickly. Tomorrow if we can."

"We? Did the T-person say *we?*"

"I couldn't work it without you, Ahmad. You give dignity and credibility to deception. Also, every movie

I've ever seen has G-men and T-people working in pairs. Any kid knows that!"

"Seems like the older I get, the dumber I get. Tomorrow's out. Old Anse will need a day to research a little, a snap of you, and a couple hours to make his layout. I'll call him when I get up and have him meet me for lunch maybe. Saturday would be a better day for this anyway. Government doesn't want to embarrass Mr. Harvey in front of his employees, you know. Very considerate, government is, because, you know, it's Harvey's government as well as yours and mine. You can stall off Squires, I imagine, if you try. Got the notion he's kinda sweet on you, honey. That's why he treats you so tough."

"Uh-huh."

"He'll be coming over tomorrow, I guess, to pick up your telephone tape."

"Why do you guess that?"

"Could have had the lab man pick it up with the crowbar, couldn't he?"

"Well, yes, but the lab's not in Civic Center Complex."

"He'll come himself. Don't doubt my credibility. Now I need some sleep."

"How're you doing with B. T.?"

"Okay. Tell you tomorrow. I'll call 'bout one. After I see Anse. You know where he's at, and he'll tell me when he wants you for the picture. Be there when I call."

Ahmad hung up.

I turned off the light and tried to sleep some more, but I couldn't. I felt as if I had just drunk a pot of a hundred percent caffeine-full coffee, and after ten or fifteen minutes, I got up and brewed a pot of coffee to calm my nerves.

16

Anse's Wide World Print Shop occupies a thirty-foot storefront building on Fenkell Avenue near Greenfield Road, a district which thirty years ago was an upper-class neighborhood of brick homes. White occupants making twenty to forty thousand dollars a year lived more or less happily here, supporting the pizzerias, hardware stores, bars, barbershops, drugstores, and doctors' and dentists' offices that were the businesses along the neighborhood's main artery, Fenkell Avenue. Today, as in scores of similar areas throughout the northwest section of Detroit, urban blight has set in like a contagious fungus: lawns lie unweeded, unseeded, and unfertilized; half the street lights on residential avenues have been stoned out, and the residents, now ninety percent black, will not walk half a block unac-companied. In the alleys between streets, abandoned wheel-stripped cars make the passage of sanitation trucks impossible, and people must cart their refuse to the front curbs on pick-up day, so that the rats are as comfortable on main streets as in alleys.

I had no sooner manipulated my car into a slot two storefronts down from Wide World than two lithe black youths wearing jeans and blue jackets approached my car, one from the street side, the other on the sidewalk. Both were smiling broadly, and I was able to slip Snubby from my purse into the side pocket of my coat before one, a boy of perhaps fifteen but already six feet tall, leaned down to my side window and shouted in to me, "Mistah Dakah sent us."

I unlocked the door and stepped out.

"Don't you worry none 'bout yoh cah, Ma'am," he said. "We'll look out foah it."

If I were an artist, I think Anse would be the subject of more than one of my paintings. Neither white nor black, a slender reed of a man perhaps five and a half feet tall, with knobby elbows and knuckles and a face skull-thin beneath a jungle of curly battleship-gray hair, somehow he seems to me to be a summation of the griefs of the ages. Nor is his ascetic aspect belied by his behavior. He rarely speaks, conducting conversations in the main with nods and gestures.

"What is he?" I asked Ahmad after I first met Anse. "A Moor?"

"Fulani."

"Which is?"

"The Fulani are a people who have been roaming around in the Senegal-Sudan area of North Africa since prebiblical times. They know how to live in the desert as frugally as camels, but they have a sense of loyalty to their tribe that would put an old Scots clansman to shame. He lives pretty much on herbal teas and bread."

"How did he happen to come here?"

"Some day, if I ever get him to trust me fully, I'm going to ask him that question. Right now, it would be an arrogance to ask."

Anse is a faultless printer and an artist with etchings on either plate or woodblock. Before every Christmas he makes a new etching depicting a desert scene not unsuggestive of the Magi's journey, and sells five hundred at fifteen dollars apiece. The first two hundred go out by mail to subscribers who collect his work. The rest are sold to passersby who see the etching in his store window. If any previous years' editions are left over, he displays them as well, priced at twelve dollars each. Old Anse has a merry Christmas every year, I imagine, whatever his own religion may be.

He was expecting me, and ushered me beyond the order counter into the rear. He gestured me to a worn overstuffed armchair, shuffled out of sight beyond a velveteen drape into what I assumed were his personal quarters, and emerged shortly with a demitasse of very strong ginseng tea, which he handed to me with the suggestion of a smile on his leathery lips. Then he returned to a workbench on which were banks of pens, pencils, chalks, several small cameras, three pairs of shears, and other miscellany related to his various trades as photographer, printer, artist. Perhaps fifteen minutes after I sat down, he beckoned me to stand before a green-tinted wall with my feet touching a line painted on the floor.

"No smile," he said, and his voice was a high-register tenor.

He took two snapshots of me, waved me back to the chair, and while the photos were airing dry, he brought me a wallet-size piece of thin cardboard with as official a bureau identification write-up as I've ever seen, complete with a Washington, D.C. verification telephone number printed in very small type at the bottom of the card.

"Picture go here," he said, pointing to a blank square at the left of the card.

He worked ten more minutes, and when he returned, the write-up complete with picture had been transformed into a plastic card.

"Very, very good!" I said, and handed him the envelope in which I had put two fifties and five twenties before I had left my apartment. "And thank you for the tea. It was excellent."

He escorted me to the door, where one of the black lads in jeans was waiting. The other was leaning against my car, but seeing me, he hurried to the street door so that he could open it for me when I produced my key.

"Thank you," I said to them when I was ready to start the engine. "And thank Mr. Dakar for me, please."

It was three-thirty when I got back home, and I immediately called Charlotte Harvey, who said she was making after-school sandwiches for the children.

"What time does Emmett go to his office on Saturday?" I asked her.

"Different times," she said. "It depends on what the children have planned."

"But he's likely to go sometime, isn't he?"

"Yes. He didn't always used to, but for the last four months or so he always goes. I don't think he wants to be alone with me."

"Call me when he leaves for the office tomorrow, please."

"Where? At the office?"

"No. Here at my home. I want to talk to him privately. I want to surprise him with some information that may help solve your problem. No promises on that, but hope. I can't explain it now. But you will call me the minute he leaves, won't you?"

"Of course. Oh, I hope this will all be over soon."

There was nothing else I could do today. Ahmad was somewhere with B. T. Hickory doing whatever Hickory was paying him to do. I changed into jeans and a sweater, and was actually closing my apartment door on the way to Moffat's when the telephone called me back inside. It was Jim Squires.

"Where you been?" he demanded. "I've been calling all afternoon."

"I'm so sorry!" I replied. "I apologize, Lieutenant. I was out earning a living, but if I'd any idea you were going to call, well, of course I would have stayed here and knitted all day long."

"Knock it off, J. D. Listen. I want that tape. I'll bring a machine and record what Jenkins said. We don't need your tape. You gonna be there in fifteen minutes?"

"I'll be here."

And in exactly twelve and one half minutes, Jim was "here" with me.

It's strange how subject we are to suggestion—I assume that I am more or less typical of the human race. I have known Jim Squires for almost six years, having first bumped into him on one of my earliest retrievals—a five-thousand-dollar diamond bracelet stolen from one of Southfield's charitable black matrons while she was attending a benefit for the Southfield Little Symphony Orchestra. The thief was another charitable matron, a white bigot whose motive was to discourage what she termed, at the height of her hysteria, "nigger participation in cultural affairs." I presented the evidence to Jim, who then was still a sergeant handling robberies and B. & E.s, and I went with him when he made the arrest. Later I met his wife Shirley, a quiet all-suffering type of unliberated house-marm, and a year or so ago, like many other people, I was surprised when she sued successfully for divorce. But my relationship with Jim, though generally cordial, has always been professional, and I respected him as an efficient and thorough policeman, and thought that he considered me an intelligent and often useful retriever who sometimes simplified the work of local police forces.

All this being so, why now should I be nervous about letting Jim into my apartment just because of an off-hand remark by Ahmad? Ahmad had lots of "notions" that turned out to be nonsense, didn't he? Oh, yes—but more that were as right as geometric propositions.

"Nice place you got here," Jim said after I hung his coat in the closet. "What you have to pay for a place in this building?"

157

"Depends. The higher it is the more expensive. That's why I'm only on the third floor. You want some coffee?"

"How about a drink?"

"On duty, Lieutenant?"

"I'm off at four, which it will be by the time you mix me a bourbon and soda. I figure you must have bourbon, since that's what Dakar drinks."

"He drinks Jack Daniel's black sour mash. Will that do?"

"If it's good enough for him, I guess I can stand it," he said, sitting down in the armchair alongside my telephone.

I mixed him a drink, very weak on bourbon, very long on soda, and poured myself a glass of Diet Coke. By the time I was finished, he had set up his recorder to tape my tape.

"Turn her on," he said, and I did.

He played his copy back to make sure it had taken clearly, then leaned back in the chair and took a long draught of the bourbon-flavored soda.

"You know, J. D.," he said, "I'm going the extra mile for you."

"Oh? Well, I appreciate all favors, Jim, even when I don't know what they are."

He grunted.

"You know damn well I could have got a court order making you tell me the name of your client. And this tape here—you don't think I believe for one minute that you haven't known about it all along."

"As I said, I appreciate all favors, Jim. But I feel obliged to point out that even if you had gotten a court order, you couldn't have made me reveal the name of my client. And as for the tape—I told you about it and here you are recording it."

He didn't press the issue, but downed some more of his drink as if it was water.

"D.A.'s office tells me you've arranged to get counsel for Janescu. You want to tell me why?"

"Of course. Because I'm convinced the man did not kill Harry."

"We got him dead to rights. Janescu's lighter in Jenkins's pocket, bit of Jenkins's trouser-tear in the trunk of Janescu's car."

"You don't really believe that a murderer would leave his cigarette lighter in his victim's pocket, do you?"

"Well, he mighta loaned it sometime before and then forgot who he gave it to. Lighters are cheap as matches today."

"That was no cheap flic-a-Bic, Jim. It was a gift to Janescu from one of his managers. Gold-plated, French-made. A hundred dollar lighter these days with R. J. initialled on each side. A memento dear to Rick's heart."

"Janescu used to be a prizefighter. You know that?"

"Yes. And a very good one."

"So he's probably punchy. He didn't expect to be associated with the killing. Punchy guys are like old people. They forget details. It'll stand up in court."

"If it ever gets there, which I doubt."

Jim finished his drink, held his glass up to the light, then looked at his watch.

"Way past four now. Think you could spare me another drink?"

I looked at my own watch.

"One more," I said. "I'm meeting some friends at Moffat's in a few minutes."

"Make this one half and half, please."

I switched to a lowball glass, and poured a drink that was pretty much on the rocks. Jim took a sip, swallowed, then ahhed.

"More like it," he said, settling into the armchair. "Something I been meaning to ask you for a long time.

I know the J stands for Jane. What's the D stand for?"

"Dainty," I said.

He studied my face a few seconds, unsure whether I was serious.

"C'mon," he said.

"It doesn't have to stand for anything, Jim. Lots of people have middle initials that don't stand for anything."

"Then why have them?"

"Well, can you imagine anyone calling me just J?"

"That's a man's name."

"See? So I use J. D. so people won't think I'm a man."

"Nobody'd make that mistake, believe me, Jane."

It was the first time he had ever used my given name, and ten warning buoys popped up in my mind. Chart a safe course, J. D., I advised myself: the channel between offending and being offended is crooked and narrow.

"You know I've been divorced?" Jim asked, *à propos de bottes, comme on dit en français,* a favorite expression of my Michigan French professor when he wanted to change the subject in his conversational French class.

"I heard. Sorry."

"No need to be. We didn't fit. Shirley was all right, but she wasn't meant to be a cop's wife, if you know what I mean."

I didn't reply.

"You ever been married, Jane?"

"No."

"Must have had a few offers in your time."

"Dozens, Jim. But I'm not the marrying kind."

"Ah, c'mon. Unnatural for a woman not to want to be married. To the right guy, I mean. A healthy woman, not a dike."

"No more unnatural than for a man. A man who doesn't want to be married occupies himself, presumably, with other matters—his work, his hobby, sports—whatever. The same applies to unmarried women."

"Except for one thing. Sex."

"What's that got to do with it? Sex is sex whether you're married or not."

"Yeah, guess that's true today all right. But didn't used to be."

"You want to turn back the clock, Jim? Bring back all the phony Victorian standards?"

"They weren't so phony. You didn't have half the kids in the country bastards, way it is today. You know how many unmarried mothers are on A.F.D.C. in Oakland County alone? Jesus! And when you get to Wayne County I guess there's twice as many. Government's supporting fifteen, twenty percent of the kids in this country with tax dollars."

I glanced at my watch.

"I don't doubt you're right, Jim, but at least they're being supported instead of starving or, worse, abandoned. Really, I must leave. I'm a little late already."

"Okay," he said, and took a long swallow of his drink.

I got his coat from the closet. The sky was dark, and a few odd snowflakes were bouncing in the wind-patterns outside my window.

"You still going steady with that lawyer?" Jim asked as I held his coat and he wriggled into it.

"More with him than with anyone else."

"Maybe sometime, if I give you notice, you and me could go someplace. Have dinner, maybe, at some supper club, huh?"

"Maybe, but not till this case is over."

"What's that got to do with it?"

"I never date anyone connected with a case I'm working on. It's unprofessional and unethical."

"Huh," he muttered, "except Dakar."

I preferred not to hear this remark.

161

17

When I went to Moffat's that late Friday afternoon, I had every intention of drinking two of Milt Prudhomme's Margaritas—his proportions suit me precisely—then of eating a light dinner, whitefish almondine, perhaps, with a glass of some German Moselle. I intended to get home early for an hour of relaxation and a solid night's sleep.

I got the dinner and the sleep, but it was nearly midnight when I trundled in, awash inside with eight or nine or who-cares-how-many glasses of Moselle, Bernkastle, Chenin Blanc, chablis, blanc de blanc—the only requirement for our table of seven sturdy ladies was that the wine be white and different from the previous order. I hadn't had a Friday evening with what Milt calls "Moffat's Choir Girls" since late spring. I had spent a month and a half of midsummer in Traverse City working on the troublesome but ultimately solvable theft of two miniature Chagalls—the brother-in-law did it and hid the pictures in his locker at his country club. Then after a little vacation in Colorado, the Winkler woman's disappearance took me to Florida, and when I returned I wasn't in the mood or the physical condition for light-hearted career-woman dalliance at Moffat's or anywhere else, because I looked a sight with my blackened eyes and puffed-up cheeks.

But I had missed the infrequent but full-of-fun-and-fury sessions with pudgy Norma Healy, who told exaggerated tales of the advances of lustful purchasing agents; Selma Gideon, thrice-divorced, who measured men against the worse traits of her three exes; Jackie and Bernice Truran, twin sisters in the flesh, each weighing "somewhere between 110 and 200 pounds," both grade school teachers who claimed they spent half their waking hours protecting their charges from the demands of parents who insisted their children were "gifted"; Aimee Dupres, sleek, svelte, and sarcastic, who carried a business card which read, beneath her name, "National Bank of Detroit's Birmingham Token Black Beauty"; and rich Christine "Christy" Mathierson, past forty and the oldest of our group, divorced from a retired G.M. executive twice her age, self-described as "career debauchée." We never planned our meetings and sometimes the group was only four or five. But when all seven of us happened to get together, somehow bottles multiplied, laughter became raucous, and Milt would banish us to the big balcony's round booth, where we couldn't be seen and could be heard as in the distance. In a way, I suppose, our Friday evenings at the old watering hole might be considered another triumph for women's rights.

On Saturday morning, I was up at eight. Two cups of coffee, two glasses of orange juice, and a poached egg on toast settled my stomach, and a three-mile walk in the crisp snow-scented air cleared my head. I didn't expect Charlotte to phone till after ten o'clock, and I hoped it would be after eleven so that Ahmad could get a decent night's sleep. In the event, it was not till one-thirty, by which time Ahmad had already checked in with me, and he responded at once to my phone alert.

"I'm going to be late on the job," he said as we swung onto Maple Road heading east. "Orders were to be at the Foxes and Hounds by two."

"This won't take long," I said. "If it works. And if it doesn't, it will take only a few minutes."

"I'm not gonna ask how you plan to swing it. I know you'll surprise me. I'll just play deep safety. You're the linebacker."

"If that makes sense to you, it suits me fine," I said.

"You don't want a technical explanation of the terminology and its symbolism?"

"No way."

"Shucks!" he said, pretending to pout.

The building security guard did not come on duty till six o'clock on Saturdays, because lots of law offices and insurance firms and doctors were working full force, so we hummed right up to the fifteenth floor. The door to the office was locked, but I had my Sears, Roebuck key and quietly, we entered. I pointed past the empty reception desk to Harvey's office, in which a light glowed through the opaque glass of the door that bore his name.

"Charge!" Ahmad whispered.

I rapped three times firmly on the wood surrounding the door glass, then without waiting for recognition, opened the door and stepped as briskly as I could into the office, with Ahmad's ebony hulk right behind me. Harvey was sitting at his desk, a stack of computer printouts in front of him, one sheet still in his right hand.

"Miss Mulroy!" he said.

"Yes, Mr. Harvey. I'm afraid I have some bad news for you."

"How did you get in here? Did Essie give you a key?"

"I have a key. I'll begin by apologizing, not for being here but for deceiving you about my identity."

I clicked open my purse, drew from it my wallet, and from the wallet Anse's plastic card, which I dropped on the desk in front of Harvey. He picked it up, confused, read it, became more confused, and stared up at me holding the card in his left hand.

"Treasury Department?" he asked.

I plucked the card from his hand, and while I returned it to my purse, said, "This is Mr. Dakar, also of the Treasury Department."

Ahmad drew a leather card case from his pocket, opened it, and extended it in his huge right hand toward Harvey. The light from the desk lamp glowed on the all-purpose badge that looked so threatening when Ahmad proffered it briefly, but confidently.

"I don't understand," Harvey said.

Without an invitation, I sat down alongside his desk, then casually opened my leather underarm briefcase, drew out the copies of the SMACO transactions, and dropped them on the desk in front of Harvey. A glance told him what they were.

"Mr. Harvey, you're in deep trouble," I said.

He did not argue; his eyes were moist when he looked at me, but he said nothing.

"Do you know what the penalties can be for laundering illegal money, Mr. Harvey?"

"Laundering?"

"Reprocessing it into the economic system to make it appear to have been legally earned. As a capital gain from a stock investment, for instance. Those stock investments!" And I pointed at the SMACO accounts in front of him.

"I'm merely a broker," he said.

"You're the underwriter as well," I replied sternly. "Nobody else handles the stock. Nobody else has ever handled it. And you know why."

Harvey's facial muscles were slack now. He looked every bit as stunned and as guilty as a student who, having successfully plagiarized for a long time, finds himself caught in the very act. Yet I think I sensed a kind of relief, an acceptance of the guilt he had been hiding for so long.

"I had to do it," he said simply.

"Nobody has to break the law," Ahmad said, and his deep voice resonated in the small office.

"Yes, I had to do it, or they would have sent me to prison for life."

"They blackmailed you into doing it?" I asked.

He nodded.

"In that case, we might be able to help you," I said. "Duress is often considered a mitigating circumstance. Tell us about it."

He uttered what might have been a laugh had it not been so bitter.

"No one can help," he said dully. "Unless you can bring the dead to life."

"You killed Harry Jenkins?"

"Who?"

Either he was a consummate actor, or he had never heard of Harry.

"Tell us about it," Ahmad interrupted, speaking more softly now. "What did they have on you?"

Harvey looked up at Ahmad for a moment. Perhaps he saw understanding in those deep dark eyes; or possibly the time had come when he no longer wanted to conceal what he had for so long kept caged inside himself.

"It began four, five months ago. I was in Vegas. I used to like to gamble. Not the machines or tables. Poker. I've always liked to play poker, since I was a kid. I was good at it and I liked it. I used to go to Vegas or Atlantic City and play poker. Not real high stakes, just the two, five, ten-dollar tables. I got to know a lot of the locals in Vegas, guys who live there, lot of them retired, who fill in the tables, you know? I kind of became one of them when I was there, sitting with them all day long because I was just as good at it as they were."

"One day this big guy came in and sat at a table where I was playing. He was on the edge of being drunk but he was jolly and had a lot of money and played his cards right. That night I hit one of those streaks that make it all seem worthwhile. He had a straight, I'd luck out with a flush. He had a little boat, I'd come in with a bigger one. Seven straight hands he had what would normally win, but I had a better hand every time. It kind of got to him and I guess with the raises and all, I must have won close to fifteen hundred from him in about half an hour.

"Finally, he threw his cards down on the table and I think he would have taken a swing at me except that this guy was with him, his bodyguard, somebody told me afterward, held him back."

Harvey stopped talking to collect his thoughts, then looked up at us, his eyes moving from my face to Ahmad's, and back to mine, and I feared for an instant that he was having second thoughts about what he was doing.

"Go on," Ahmad said softly, sitting on the side of Harvey's desk.

"Well, next day I got on the plane to come back home, and I'd won a couple of thousand dollars all told, so I changed my ticket from coach to first class because I wanted to see what it was like, and right across the aisle from me there was this big guy and his buddy."

"Mr. B. T. Hickory," I said.

"That's right! How do . . ."

"Never mind. Go on, please."

"He was sober now, and friendly. 'Sorry about last night,' he said to me. 'You got lucky and I got drunk. Hope to play with you again so I can get even. Where you going?' Turned out he was from Southfield, and he asked me my business. He said he owned a lot of bonds and stocks, and maybe we could do business sometime. So I gave him my card—you know how it goes on planes to pass the time.

"I didn't think anymore about it until maybe three weeks or so later he called me at my office and said he was having a poker game in his apartment and there was an open seat, would I like to come and give him a chance to get even. I accepted, damnit! If I hadn't I wouldn't be in this God-awful situation!"

Harvey paused, shaking his head at the memory of the greatest mistake of his life.

"How much did you lose?" Ahmad asked.

"I didn't lose. I won more than five thousand dollars. It was a lot of fun for me, since the stakes were higher than I usually play. Trouble is, I had a couple of drinks while we were playing. I don't usually drink when I play cards, fact is I don't usually drink anything but maybe a glass of wine when my wife and I go out to dinner. But there were three girls there, friends of Hickory and the other guys at the table, and they kept bringing drinks out. Hickory drinks bourbon like it was water, and he's so big it doesn't seem to affect him too much. I was winning heavy, though, and everybody else was drinking, so I took maybe three drinks, and after we quit I had another. That was the one I shouldn't have had. I got woozy and terribly sleepy, and I had this pounding headache. Hickory said I shouldn't drive, and he told one of the girls, a redhead named Cindy, to help me to a spare bedroom in his apartment. He has a three-bedroom penthouse on top of one of those golden-glass insurance company towers just off Greenfield, beautiful place with an outside patio garden.

"That's the last I remember until I woke up. I swear it is!"

He stopped and had to be prompted to continue.

"So?" I said.

"She was dead. On the floor. Most of her clothes torn off, blood all over her legs. She'd been strangled with her own brassiere!"

Harvey squeezed his eyes shut, trying to blot out the image so vivid in his imagination, as he hunched low into his swivel chair.

"And I killed her!" he finished.

"How do you know that?" Ahmad asked. "You say you don't remember anything after you passed out, then you woke up and she was dead. How do you know *you* killed her?"

"I know. There were strands of her hair stuck in my fingernails and blood on me. My trousers and shorts were lying on the floor all the way across the room, and there was blood on me, her blood—where it shouldn't be, you understand?"

"What time was it when you woke up?" Ahmad asked, thinking, I have no doubt, that because of the sexual aspect of the crime, a man would have more success interrogating than a woman.

"Ten past three."

"How do you know that?" I asked.

"I asked him."

"Hickory?"

"Yes."

"Then he was there when you woke up?"

"He woke me. Poured cold water on my face, and slapped me a couple of times to bring me to."

"Then told you that you'd killed the girl?"

"He didn't have to tell me. I could see plain enough. The smell of her perfume, Halston, was all over me. It's the same one that our receptionist uses. You know, Essie."

We sat silent for half a minute.

"Shall I turn myself in to you, or go to the Troy police?" Harvey asked.

"Neither, yet," Ahmad said. "What did you do with the body?"

"Hickory made me get up and take a shower. When I got dressed, he said he would take care of the body, and he told his bodyguard, fellow named Rick, who was sleeping in the living room, to drive me home in my car. Said a taxi would pick him up a few minutes after he got me home. I was still groggy, hardly knew what I was doing. The whole thing seemed like a bad dream that wouldn't end. I remember once or twice thinking was that what was happening to me even while it was happening."

"Exactly how long ago did all this happen, Mr. Harvey?" I asked.

"It was a Friday. Eleventh of August."

"And how did Hickory take care of the body?" Ahmad asked.

"When I talked to him next, he . . ."

"When was that?" I interposed.

"Tuesday. The next week. He called me and asked me to meet him for lunch at the Colorado Beef House. It's a restaurant off Big Beaver near Dequindre Road. The manager is a friend of his. He was in the game that night."

"That would be Terry Garfinkel?" I said.

"Him—yes. Hickory said that Terry owed him for some favors, and that he had agreed to keep the body in a freezer in the basement of the restaurant until they could figure out how to dispose of it. He said not to worry, there wouldn't be any trouble because Cindy had been a waitress in the restaurant and she didn't have any family in the area and only one sister who lived in Tacoma, Washington, whom she didn't like and who didn't like her. Terry took me down to the basement and showed me the freezer. It has a padlock on it so nobody can open it without getting the key from him."

"Did you look at the body?"

"God, no! Terry had the key and offered to let me see her, but I said no. I couldn't look at her again!"

"Is the body still there in the freezer?" I asked.

"Yes."

"That was nearly four months ago. Why hasn't Hickory gotten rid of it as he said he would?"

"He plans to wait until the real cold sets in, like in January when the lakes freeze over. Then he says he'll take it far out in Lake St. Clair, where he and some friends always have an ice-fishing shelter, and slip it into the water. It won't be found until the spring thaw, and by then the fact that the body was once frozen stiff will seem perfectly natural. I should never have gone along with the plan, but I have a wife and two children, and I couldn't bring myself to put them through the horror of the thing and the scandal it would create in the papers. It was wrong, I know, but I just couldn't make myself go to the police."

I had taken my wallet calendar from my purse.

"Tuesday," I said. "That would have been August fifteenth. The same day you handled the first redemption of the Southeastern Michigan Assets Company's redeemable preference stock."

"Yes. Hickory asked me to handle it since I was in the business."

"And you've handled all the subsequent redemptions?"

"Yes."

"Where did the money for the redemptions come from?"

"Terry Garfinkel always had company checks all properly made out to the recipients, and receipts."

"Who signed the checks?"

"The company president and treasurer."

"That would be Mr. Wilfred Tattersby and Terry's wife, Nancy Ann?"

"Is she his wife?"

"Haven't you met her?"

"No."

"Mr. Tattersby?"

"No."

"Who handled the original purchases of the stock at one dollar a share?"

"Nobody handled them, I guess. Hickory told me to make out confirmations of purchases and back-date them to January 2. I did that, though I knew it was illegal."

"Didn't that markup seem absurdly high to you? Buy at one dollar, sell seven months later at one hundred dollars? Instant IBM original stock profit in only seven months' time?"

"I didn't think much of anything at the time. Later, I realized it was suspicious. But I was merely a broker supervising the sale. I wasn't doing anything illegal handling the redemptions. And I was paid the proper commissions."

"But you suspected that there must be something illegal about what your clients were doing."

"I guess so."

"Tell me, Mr. Harvey," Ahmad took over the interrogation, "did you take that five thousand dollars you won at Hickory's apartment home with you the night you played poker and killed the girl?"

"No. I forgot about it. I don't think I would have wanted it anyway."

"So what happened to it?"

"Hickory said he gave it to Terry. For keeping the body."

"Pretty high price for a little electricity," Ahmad said. "You wait right here, Mr. Harvey. Miss Mulroy and I want to have a little private conference."

He moved toward the door and I followed, but before we went into the outer office, he turned back toward Harvey.

"You cooperate with us," he said, "as you've been doing right now, and things may not be as bad as you think."

Outside he spoke very softly.

"They've played him for a patsy," he said. "He never killed that girl."

"You think they killed her just to trap him?"

"If they wanted her dead, they'd do it, sure. But maybe she's not dead. He didn't give her a medical when he saw her there—you can bet on that. Look. I'm almost an hour late. Only reason we'll be drinking at the Foxes and Hounds is that the Beef House doesn't open on Saturdays till four. But we'll be there sometime after that, and then I want a look in that freezer. You get in touch with Jim, give him a rundown, and he can get someone from the Troy station to meet him there. Say about five. I gotta go."

"What about Harvey?"

"Tell him to go home and wait."

I lingered a little before returning to Harvey's office, trying to decide whether to tell him of his wife's role in his present predicament, and decided not to. His actions had been foolish, if not criminal, and a brief interim of desperate concern over the prospect of imminent discovery seemed a proper penance for his folly. Besides, if the entire episode could be concealed from his wife and her sister, he would be better off in the long run.

He was still at his desk when I returned, but was not handling printouts now.

"Mr. Harvey," I said, "I want you to go home and stay there so that we can get in touch with you when we want to. Say nothing to anybody about this—not even to your wife. Do you understand?"

"But . . ."

"You do intend to cooperate with us, don't you?"

"Yes, but . . ."

"No *buts!* Complete silence. Agreed?"

"Yes, of course."

18

If I had done what Ahmad had suggested, probably everything would have turned out as we hoped. The trouble began when I started to think of ways to certify a happy ending.

Suppose, J. D., I thought, just suppose that you call Jim and he and his men, along with some Troy officers, turn up about five. You tell them, "The body of a murdered girl has been freezing in the basement of this restaurant for four months. Want to see?" They commandeer the key, we troupe into the basement, the freezer is opened to reveal—what? Sides of pork? Veal roasts? Yummy-yum-yum frozen tart desserts?

Not a pretty picture for the astute Mulroy to contemplate. One reputation vastly diminished. Possibility of slander suits from restaurant owner, Garfinkel himself, and SMACO right in your face, Mulroy! Shouldn't you make certain there's really a body in that freezer before you get the police involved? I asked myself. Or, if you can't get into the freezer, shouldn't you confirm that there really was a waitress named Cindy working at the Beef House four or five months ago? Myself nodded yes.

It was seven minutes before four when I pulled into the Colorado Beef House parking lot, one of three cars in the guest area. I considered waiting till four exactly, then decided that was foolish. The one person who would know about Cindy would be Nanette, the hostess, who acted as if she had been at her job before the first dollar had been taken in and framed. It would be best to catch her before she got busy. I could maybe buy her a drink while we chatted girl-to-girl. She could hardly refuse to talk to Cindy's sister from Tacoma, could she? Even if no Cindy had ever worked here, it would be simple common decency to reassure a searching sister.

Nanette doubled as hostess and coat-check girl until the dinner crowd began to arrive about six. She was busy realigning the numbers of the hangers in the coat closet so that they would be in proper sequence when I appeared. Smiling, she came to me, then seeing no one with me, the smile faded.

"Hi!" I said.

"Hello," she said. "You alone?"

She didn't seem to recognize me, or if she did, saw no reason to make a point of it.

"I'm expecting some friends later on," I said. "I'll just sit at the bar till they get here. And? . . ."

"Yes?"

"If you have a moment, I'd like to talk to you. When you're finished with what you're doing. Maybe I could buy you a drink."

"Too early for me, dear. Something special you want to talk about?"

"My sister. She used to work here."

Two men swung into the restaurant, shaking the cold from their shoulders.

"You go along. I'll find you when I get a minute," Nanette said, turning to the new arrivals with a full-incisor smile and a gay "Hi there!"

I sat discreetly near the far end of the bar and waited for Lorelei to finish wiping dust and finger smudges from the front row of bar bottles. She recognized me immediately.

"Short time, no see," she said. "What'll it be? Margarita up, very little salt?"

"Not right away. I'm expecting some friends to join me and I don't want to get ahead of them, you know?"

"Do I ever!"

"A Perrier will do for now."

"Gotcha."

The Perrier and Nanette arrived at about the same time. She slid into the seat next to mine, waved Lorelei off, and faced me with no smile.

"If you're looking for a job, we're full up," she said, then added, after surveying me as a stock breeder might evaluate a bull for sale at a county fair, "but you can leave your name and number if you want to."

"No," I said. "I came about my sister, like I said. I know she was working here about six months ago. One of her friends told me that."

"What's the name?"

"She went by the name of Cindy, I understand. That's not her real name but that's what she was called here. I don't know what last name she might have given."

"Cindy?"

"Uh-huh."

"No. I been here since the opening and I don't remember any girl called Cindy. Must be some other place she worked."

"Oh," I said, assuming the sad mask of disappointment.

"Hey—I remember!" Lorelei half-shouted, turning from her bottles. "She was a cute little redhead, right?"

"Yes, that's Cindy!" I said.

"And natural, too. I thought it was a rinse at first, but then I saw her one day in the loo-loo, and there was nothing unnatural about her."

"Lorelei! When will you learn to mind your own business!" Nanette said, then added, "Oh, never mind. What was her last name? I can look up our records."

"I'm not sure what name she might have used," I answered, quite honestly. "She ran away from her husband and didn't want him ever to find her. So she probably used a false name."

"Wait a sec!" Lorelei said. "Cindy—Cindy—Cindy Schumas! Or Sumac maybe. Way I remember both names began with the same letter. Maybe not letter, same sound, anyway. Ssss. See what I mean?"

"Thank you, Lorelei," Nanette said with an irony solid enough to rust.

She slipped from the bar chair.

"I'll look it up soon as I get that bunch settled," she said, returning to her station.

"Geez! Guess she didn't like Cindy," Lorelei said, moving toward the other end of the bar where the two men who had followed me in had perched after they returned from the john.

So I sat sipping my Perrier water and pretending not to dislike it, watching and waiting like the first-class operator that I am. The restaurant was coming to life, though no one was interested in food yet. Finally, Nanette was free and headed toward the kitchen, beyond which, I correctly assumed, was the office. A bulky bulging-eyed little box of a man, reeking of Brut, sat down two stools up from me, cleared his throat twice, then decided against saying whatever his usual opening gambit was. Lorelei served him, without being asked, a bottle of Heineken beer. The red-vested little Englishman whom I had met ascending from the basement worked his way beneath the immovable bar-well opening carrying a box of lowball glasses, which he systematically began lining up in the glass-washing machine.

"Good God, Willie! We don't need no more glasses!" Lorelei said in a fortissimo alto whisper.

"Mister Terry sigh ter bring 'um, so 'ere they be, Miss Lorry," Willie replied, glancing embarrassedly up at me and the Brut boy.

A middle-aged man and woman, she wearing three strands of eight-and-a-half millimeter cultivated Japanese pearls, probably more to hide the wrinkling skin of her neck than for any style objective, sat down between Brut and me. He had a vodka martini, she a Piña Colada. Nanette returned to her hostess-coat check job. I waited some more, sipping as little as I could. At last, there was a break in the flow-in, and Nanette hurried over to me.

"We have a file on Cindy Schumac," she said. "You want to see it, come with me."

We headed for the kitchen, but she turned down the washroom corridor and opened the basement doorway.

"We keep the discontinued employees' files downstairs," she said. "Be careful going down. The stairs are steep."

As if I didn't know! I wasn't wearing Cuban heels, and descending in medium-high heels wasn't easy, but I didn't have to be quiet as I clomped from one step to the next, balancing myself by holding onto the wobbly wooden plank that passed as a railing. I was three steps from the bottom when the flash seared through my head and tingled down my spine, my knees gave way, and I soared into the space of unconsciousness.

When I next was aware of myself and of the pulsing pain that ran from the top of my head through my neck into a pit between my shoulders, I thought for a moment that I had been buried in a truckload of straw. The odor was unmistakable—straw and dirt. I was bound at ankles and wrists, my hands crossed at my buttocks. A damp towel that smelled of detergent was knotted in my open mouth and tied behind my neck. Whenever I tried to wriggle, needles of straw would prick my body. Finally, as my head and vision cleared, I detected a haze of dimness seeping through my wrapping and I realized that I was rolled up in a piece of floor matting, the type used by establishments for people to wipe their feet on in winter weather before moving into stores or schools, or, in my case, restaurant kitchens. Dim thumps and clicks on some other nearby planet suggested to my waking brain that I was still in the basement of the Beef House.

Even a few moments of unconsciousness, like sleep or total meditation, detaches one from time. I had no idea whether I had been out for ten minutes or ten hours. A horrible idea occurred to me. After the restaurant closed for the night, was I scheduled to be strangled and frozen in a freezer until January made depositing me in a watery grave practicable? Two girls drowned in the middle of Lake St. Clair was more credible than one really, because the Coast Guard was always issuing warnings about the danger of sailing or motor boating on the big lake alone. This idea was followed by another thought even more horrible to contemplate: why hadn't I taken Ahmad's advice and telephoned Jim before I came here?

Then there were the sounds of feet descending the stairs. I heard the rasp of metal sliding against metal. There were a couple of grunts as I was lifted, carried, set down, lifted, tilted, slung, pushed, tucked at both ends, and thunked into pitch black. A motor came alive, thrumming vibrations through me, and I smelled gasoline vapors as I jolted backward with the car's initial momentum. I was in the trunk of an automobile moving only God and the driver knew where, and there was nothing, absolutely nothing, I could do about it. I lost consciousness again.

When I came to, there was a different sense of motion. I was suspended in space, still—yet moving. I could detect someone above me breathing, and I, in my packaging, moved gently with each breath, like a little boat with the ripples on a quiet lake. Suddenly motion stopped, there was the unmistakable sound of elevator doors sliding open, and I was being carried forward, then gently laid down on the floor.

"Some bundle." Ahmad's deep voice came muffled through my straw sarcophagus. "Feels like a body in there."

"Bright boy, ain't he, boss," a high-pitched raspy voice, which I was to find out belonged to Tiny Tim, said.

"Shut up," a heavier voice, which I properly assumed to be Hickory's, answered. "Lemme see what's in her purse."

Less than a minute later, he said, "Christ! No wonder Tate was mad! Roll her out of there."

My world whirled as my arms and legs were pricked and scratched in hundreds of places, but when I opened my eyes I found myself staring up into six eyes, only two of which I trusted.

"Another she-cop!" Hickory said. "They must be growin' them on trees these days, like oranges."

Tiny Tim stooped low over me, a leering grin on his bony face. He flipped my skirt up over my hips.

"She's a woman all right," he said. "All the way."

Ahmad snapped my skirt back to its proper place.

"What's goin' on here?" he demanded of Hickory. "I told you I wouldn't work for you if you're into drugs or numbers. So if she's a cop, why are you scared of her?"

"Take it easy, Dakar," Hickory said. "I didn't lie to you. I'm just doing a favor for a friend who she might be able to damage. It's got nothing to do with you. She'll never tell anyone you carried her up here."

"I damn well wouldn't have if you'd told me what I was carrying. I should have figured it out when you insisted on using the freight elevator."

Hickory was bending over me now, studying my face.

"Seems like I've seen her before," he said, then added, speaking to me, "If I take the gag out, will you promise not to scream?"

I jerked my head forward and he lowered himself to my side with the agility of an elephant kneeling.

When he was unknotting the towel, he said, "Wouldn't make any difference if you did scream. We're on top of the building and these walls are just about sound-proof to keep out the rock-and-roll beats."

He clambered to his feet, breathing hard.

"Put her in that armchair, Dakar," he said.

Ahmad lifted me as if I were a feather pillow, and when his back was turned on Hickory, winked down at me. He settled me sedately in a velveteen upholstered armchair.

I sat inhaling great gobs of air unfiltered by a damp soapy towel, and exercising my tongue, which had gone numb, by running it along my teeth and the roof of my dry mouth.

"What are you planning to do with her?" Ahmad asked.

"Not for me to say," Hickory answered.

Tim laughed.

"We got to do her same as the other one," he said.

"Shut your mouth!" Hickory snapped.

He faced me.

"So you're from the Treasury Department," he said. "Mind telling me what you're trying to prove?"

"Can I have a glass of water?" I asked, and my voice sounded far off to my ears. "My mouth is very dry."

"Get her some water, Dakar," Hickory said, and Ahmad went out of the room into what I presumed was the kitchen.

"What about him?" Tim said in a semiwhisper the instant Ahmad was out of hearing. "He won't go along with doing her."

"Wait for Tate. He'll decide."

Ahmad returned with a glass of water, which he held to my lips while I sipped, stopped sipping, then sipped much more.

"I wish someone would tell me what *you're* trying to prove," I said then to Hickory. "Yes, I'm with the Treasury Department. So what? I check out people who file suspicious income tax reports. But I'm not on duty when I go to a restaurant for a drink and a meal. So why am I here?"

"Because you got nosy about Cindy Schumac, that's why, dear lady."

"Schumac? Was that the last name she was using?"

"It was her true name," Hickory said, "as you very well know. Six years an undercover cop for the D.E.A. You assigned to drug enforcement, too? Special assignment maybe? Investigate disappearance of a sister cop?"

"I'll say no more until my attorney arrives," I said.

Miraculously, as if in response to my need, a buzzer sounded, announcing a visitor in the viewing lobby.

"That'll be Tate," Hickory said.

He moved to a small viewing screen set in the wall near the doorway and snapped it on, then pressed a button to open the lobby door.

"Who's this guy Tate?" Ahmad asked.

"The friend I'm doing a favor for," Hickory answered.

"Wilfred J. Tattersby," I said boldly.

"You've done your homework, haven't you?" Hickory said. "Not that it will do you any good. Let him in, Tim."

Tim opened the front door just as the elevator doors slid apart, and in walked a stooped elderly man in a dirty trench coat, whose face it took me a moment to recognize: Willie, the red-vested busboy-handyman of the Beef House!

He walked over to me, stared a moment, then took off his coat: he was still wearing the red vest. From the pocket of the coat he drew a Colt .357 Magnum with a four-inch barrel.

" 'As she talked?" he asked Hicory. " 'Ow much she know?"

"She knows your name."

"She know 'ow we work it?"

"I don't know."

They talked as if I weren't present, so I decided to remind them.

"Yes, we know how you work it. We know all about your Southeastern Michigan Assets laundering operation, too. I'd suggest that you let me use the phone to call my office before my partner, who followed you here, calls in. It might go a little easier on you if they don't find me tied up like this."

"Someone been following you, Tate?" Hickory asked.

"She's bloofin', ya fool!"

"But she knew your name. We didn't mention it to her—she came right out with it on her own. And she knows about the company."

"We'll find oot soon enough. Give 'em 'alf an 'oor."

Tattersby tossed his coat on one end of a davenport and sank into the cushions at the other end. He settled the Magnum in his lap, then stared up at Ahmad, who was sitting on the arm of the chair in which he had propped me.

"Tell me aboot 'im," he said to Hickory, pointing at Ahmad.

"He's taken Rick's job. He just drives for me is all. I haven't told him anything about your business. You want I should send him home?"

"Air you gonna carry thet bundle oot 'a 'ere? 'E's your mooscle, you're givin' 'im good money fer using mooscle, make 'im airn it."

"You expect me to use any muscle, Shorty, you better talk to me 'aboot it,' not to Hickory," Ahmad said, rising to his full height, his hands on his hips. "Name's Dakar. I'm not looking for any trouble with the law, so I don't want to know what your business might be. Matter of fact, I'm not very happy with what I see goin' on here right now, so if it's all the same to you, I'm leaving."

Tattersby's right hand moved and fitted around the butt of his gun.

"You'll leave, big mon, when I sigh you do. You work fer 'ickory, you work fer me. Got it?"

Ahmad stood hesitant, measuring the four yards that separated him from the gun.

"Go ahead, tough guy, take it away from him," Tim's thin voice rasped.

Ahmad sat down on the arm of my chair again.

"I didn't bargain for this kind of risk," he said.

"Nobody expects this kind o' risk," Tattersby said. "You'll git extra pay fer extra risk. You kin coont on it."

A heavy silence sank over the room.

19

A strange vigil we kept there, with myself the only one who knew how it must end. Even Ahmad half-expected that Squires and his forces would find us. How could he know that I hadn't called Jim Squires? We sat for maybe three minutes in total silence. Then Hickory said, "I'm going to get a drink. Anybody else want one?"

"Make mine cognac," I said, and Tiny Tim giggled.

Hickory went to a sidebar along one wall and mixed himself a stiff bourbon and soda.

"Hey, boss," Tim said, suddenly earnest. "We got some time to kill before we do her. No reason why a guy can't give the little lady one last thrill before she konks for good. Lemme take her in the bedroom and give it to her."

"Sheeit, little man. She'd squeeze you to death," Ahmad said.

Suddenly Tim whipped the little pearl-handled twenty-two from its shoulder holster, cocked it, and held it two feet in front of Ahmad's groin. I believe he would have shot if Tattersby hadn't said matter-of-factly, "Shoot and I'll kill you."

The Magnum was in his hand and pointed at Tim's back.

"I was just gonna cut down Big Dick a few inches," Tim said, turning slowly but holstering his toy.

"You know, Tate, it's not a bad idea, screwing her first," Hickory said. "You read every other day about some woman found in Detroit strangled and hidden in a field or some park bushes, and almost always the autopsies show they've been raped before they were killed. Good looker like this one, whose job takes her in lots of bars at night—hey, dump her naked down in Palmer Park someplace, or over by the railroad tracks in Ferndale, nobody would think it was her job got her killed. Cops'll all blame some hop-headed jig for doing it."

"That's right!" Tim said with enthusiasm. "An' I know just the spot, too!"

"Anuther cemetery, you fool!" Tattersby said, but the expression on his face made it plain that he was considering the idea.

I began to feel like a lamb listening to picnickers debating whether to roast it whole on a spit or butcher it for chops and shanks.

"Awl right. We can't keep 'er like t'other one," Tattersby concluded. "Do it."

His grip on the Magnum had loosened but he still held it in his right hand.

"Any oobjecshun, Big Mon?" he asked Ahmad.

Ahmad's hand slipped down into my hair, then slid along my neck and began fondling my right breast.

"Not if I get first hump," he said.

"It was my idea!" Tim objected.

"You carry her in ter the bed, Timmy, you kin be ferst," Tattersby said, and I think he smiled, though it was difficult to tell.

Ahmad swung around in front of me and lifted me into his arms as easily as if I were a balloon-woman.

"First white meat you ever tasted," Tim said as we moved toward a corridor onto which the bedrooms opened.

"We'll gi' yuh fifteen minutes, no more," Tattersby called after us.

Ahmad carried me into the bedroom and laid me on the bed. Then he shut the door, plucked a straight-backed chair from in front of a vanity, and propped it tightly against the door handle. I lay looking up at a ceiling that was nearly all mirror, subdued by a tint of blue-green. Ocean blue-green seemed to have been the decorator's color motif for the room. Carpeting, drapes, wallpaper—all background features were some shade of blue-green. The upholstery, bedspread, and furniture, on the other hand, were all shades of cream-white. The effect of the decor, I imagined—at least in the decorator's mind—was the tranquility of sails on a calm sea.

But I felt anything but calm as I lay looking up at Ahmad, who stood alongside me now with an expression he was trying to project as a lustful grin.

"Never thought we'd come to this," he whispered. "But a man's gotta do what The Man says gotta be done."

"Cut me loose," I whispered back. "My hands are numb."

From the pit of his inside coat pocket he took the narrow two-inch blade pocketknife that he always carries with him, and the razor-sharp knife edge freed me in seconds. He sat down on the bedside and began rubbing my ankles while I massaged my wrists. Suddenly, he stood up, then with all his weight dropped back down on the bed.

"Scream a little," he whispered. "We got to play this one out."

I was in a mood for screaming.

"Don't you dare!" I shouted.

Brilliant J. D. Mulroy, capable of handling all crises, large and small, of protecting clients' reputation at all costs, of disdaining the advice of attorneys and police-men who enjoyed her company, of ignoring telephones!

"No! No! Don't! You son-of-a-bitch! Don't!" I screamed some more, while Ahmad continued to bounce rhythmically up and down on the springy mattress.

Finally he slowed down the rhythm, and turning serious, asked, "Think you can handle the little one if I send him in?"

"Nothing I'd like better."

"He'll have to take off the holster and his shoes and trousers before he moves on you."

"Like you did?"

"I carry a knife but never a gun," he whispered back. "Let him get ready, lie still, hands behind you, as if they're still tied. Then when he jumps you . . ."

"Right. What will you be doing? That Magnum's no cap pistol and he seems to know how to use it."

"Tell you later, when I know myself. Make sure that Tim's out cold so he can't holler for help. Then you stay here till I come get you."

He glanced at his watch. His fifteen minutes were just about up. He gestured me to lie down again, and I did with my hands behind my back. He considered my posture.

"Better take off your panties and the pantyhose," he said. "Got to make this look real."

Being a gentleman, he turned his back while I did as he asked. He took my pantyhose and stretched them out on the carpet. My panties he dropped a yard inside the doorway, as if they had been thrown there from the bed. Once again he considered my posture, then he bent my left knee, pulled the leg up a bit, and raised my skirt high on my thighs.

"The blouse," he said. "Unbutton it, take off the brassiere and drape it somewhere obvious. I got an idea little Tim is more interested in tits than ass."

While I was doing this, Ahmad said, "You never did call Jim Squires, did you?"

"I was going to call him from the restaurant. But I wanted to make certain first that there really was a Cindy, that it wasn't a hoax-murder to trap Harvey into brokering for them."

I resumed my fate-worse-than-death posture on the bed, and finally satisfied, Ahmad pointed to the pressure point beneath his Adam's apple, removed the chair from the door, unzipped his fly, took off his jacket and slung it over his left arm, pulled his shirt loosely above his belt on one side, gave me a thumbs-up sign and a smile, then opened the door and swung out of the room.

"Next!" I heard him call as he walked down the corridor to the living room.

I didn't have to wait long for my "next." He bounced into the bedroom, already removing his suit coat, and from where I was lying on the bed twenty feet from him I could smell the Brut cologne he must have slathered over his face and neck while Ahmad was presumably performing the Lord's right on me. If he was going to rape a lady, he wanted to be as chic as Cary Grant's product could make him. I moaned a little as he approached, seemed to struggle against my bonds, then sank back, resigned.

He stood a few moments taking in the scene, the panties near the door, the pantyhose on the carpet by the bed, my brassiere draped over the nightstand. Then he closed the door, took off his shoes, and unbuckled his belt. His shorts came off with his trousers, which he draped over the back of the chair Ahmad had used as a doorstop.

"I hope that your gun explodes and shoots off your balls!" I said.

Somebody had to remind him to take the holster off. He grinned, revealing a gold-capped incisor, snapped the holster button loose, and slung holster and gun onto a closet doorknob. Then he came at me, already erect.

Ahmad's guess had been right: he stretched out on top of me so that his face was above my breasts, his long-fingernailed hands working at the buttons of my blouse. I waited until he lowered his lips between my breasts and I felt his tongue tickling toward my right nipple before I seized his neck in both my hands, found the hollow beneath his Adam's apple, and pressed with both thumbs and all my might. I felt the serrations of his neckbone beneath my thumbs, and heard the gurgle at the base of his throat when he could neither swallow nor breathe. There was a spasm through his body and he collapsed, a dead weight on top of me.

I didn't know whether he was dead or not when I flopped him over onto his back, but I wasn't going to waste time in securing him. I bound his feet and hands with the same ropes that had been used on me before I felt the carotid artery for a pulse. It was there, faintly throbbing, so I hadn't quite killed him, and I was grateful for that, although I doubt any jury in the country would have convicted me under the circumstances if I *had* killed him. I pinched his nose till he groaned slightly and opened his mouth, then I jammed one of his nylon ankle-length socks into it loosely, and gagged him about the neck with a pillowcase. The entire self-salvation operation took less than five minutes, and by the time it was over, Tim was blinking his eyes and humming faint moans with every sock-filtered exhalation.

I began to put myself back together, and was drawing on my pantyhose when I felt eyes on me—whether this feeling is related to extrasensory perception or not, I can't say, but every time I have felt myself being watched intently, whether by a voyeur or some invisible sleuth assigned not to let me out of his sight, I have located the looker. Tim had managed to turn his head in my direction, and his eyes, uncomprehending yet of what they were seeing, had set on me, probably because I was the only moving object in view. I flopped him onto his stomach, checked the knots at his ankles and wrists, then, unobserved, resumed putting myself in proper order.

Satisfied if not delighted with my attire, I slipped the little pearl-handled target pistol from its holster and stood quietly against the wall next to the door, which, opening, would conceal me. I waited five, then ten minutes. Were his masters simply being extra generous with Tiny Tim? I wondered. More likely they were having difficulty deciding what was the best spot in which to dump my nude, sexually abused body. Newspaper accounts of the discovery of such victims today have become as routine as reports of head-on collisions, but in my father's time, one such discovery would have occupied police and reporters for weeks, they were so rare. Times change, morals change, a Latin poet wrote—no, it wasn't morals but mores. Same thing in the long run, I was thinking, just as I heard the explosion that could only have been the firing of the Magnum!

I had sense enough to remove my shoes before I opened the door and stepped into the corridor, gun at the ready. The carpeting was deep and padded, and I made not a whisper of a sound as I moved to the living room archway and, flattened against the wall, peeked into the room. Ahmad appeared to be sitting on the floor, his back against the davenport on which Tattersby had been sitting when I was carried off, and propped on his lap, with great gobs of blood pulsing from the blubber of his breast, was Hickory. Facing them, perhaps twelve feet away, his back toward me, was Tattersby, the gun held firmly in both his hands.

It was evident at once that, if Hickory wasn't already dead, he was surely dying. Somehow, his weight had pinned Ahmad down. I moved two silent paces toward Tattersby when he spoke.

"Yer a sunovabitch and I'm gone blow yer to kingdom come!"

Ahmad saw me and answered more loudly than was necessary.

"Won't do you no good, man, because I'm a cop and there's a stakeout outside right now. You try to leave this building without me and they'll take you dead or alive."

Six steady, quiet paces, and I was within arm's-reach of Tattersby. I snuggled the muzzle of Tiny Tim's pistol into the base of his blocked hairline, tilted slightly upward toward his brain. He could feel the cold metal against his skin.

"Drop it or die," I said as matter-of-factly as I could.

He didn't obey orders very quickly, so I increased the pressure of the muzzle against his head.

"I'll git him 'fore yew git me," Tattersby managed to mutter.

"What the fuck do I care?" I said. "You'll be doing me a favor!"

A moment later his right hand lowered and dropped the Magnum onto the carpet.

Ahmad had him trussed securely with his own belt and a bath towel two minutes later.

" 'Bout time you called Jim now, don't you think?" he asked.

"I will, as soon as you zip up your fly," I answered.

20

"You have any idea how hard it is to get at a little man sitting in the corner of a divan cuddling a Magnum in his lap?" Ahmad asked me, as we waited for the arrival of Jim Squires and whatever Troy homicide officers would be dispatched to the Southfield Tower apartment penthouse, where we sat sipping very, very old Courvoisier to protect us from the shock of Hickory's hulking death.

Ahmad had brought the tiny one into the living room, and he lay alongside the bound mastermind of the Colorado Beef House operation, Wilfred J. Tattersby. I had the decency to remove the gag from Tiny Tim's mouth, but such a stream of oaths and invectives, some involving implausible physical functions, geysered forth that Ahmad quietly regagged him.

"No way to talk in front of a lady, boy," he said.

"I tried pacing across the room," Ahmad continued, "each time coming a little closer to old Tate's couch, but when I'd get within two yards that cannon would kind of tilt toward me like I was on stage and it was my spot, you know? He didn't trust me."

Now Tattersby's eyes never left Ahmad's face, but he said absolutely nothing.

"Once I even dropped down on the other end of the couch, figuring maybe I could surprise him by suddenly whipping that center seat cushion at him, but he turned facing me, and his hand never left that gun. That's when I began wishing I hadn't told you to stay put in the bedroom. 'Mahd, man, you stooo-pid!' I told myself. 'If the situation was reversed, me in that bedroom waitin' to be attacked by some horny broad, maybe that Wagnerian alto at the Beef House, would J. D. tell me to wait in the bedroom while she took the two guys outside? No way! She believes in co-op-er-A-shun!' "

"Lucky for you the situation wasn't reversed," I said. "Lorelei would have flattened you in jig time."

"Lordy, Lordy that be the day! She can flatten me in jig time, waltz, bop, or rock time anytime! Tell the truth, though, I'm more partial to Myrna. You happen to know if she's married? We minorities, we got to stick together, you know what I mean?"

I took a long sip of cognac and rolled it slowly under my tongue. It tingled with the full burnt flavor of life here in the presence of death. I looked at Hickory propped against the couch edge where he had settled after Ahmad wriggled out from under him. But for the luck of the Irish and our own inventiveness, Ahmad could be lying there and I could be beside him, raped and strangled to death. We weren't. I was sipping the very best cognac while Ahmad was playing word games.

"You going to tell me what happened, or you want me to wait till you make a statement to the police so you won't have to repeat it?" I asked.

"I didn't finish that story, did I? Well, I got to pacing some more, then I asked Hick for a drink and he brought me a bourbon on the rocks—not my brand, Old Grand-Dad, I think it was—and time keeps wasting, slow and tedious like it always does when you're expecting action but don't know how to act. Finally, Tate looks at his watch and says, 'Time's up. Go get Tim.' He's looking at Hickory. Hick says, 'Me?' 'Yeah, you. I don't troost Big Mon.' 'Hey, I interrupt him when he's not had enough, he'll put a bullet in my belly, Tate. That boy's all balls and I'm no hand with a gun

even if I had one. You better do it. He respects you!'
"Tate considers a moment or two, then stands up.
'You sit doon 'ere,' he says to me. Here being the
couch. I do as told, Never argue with a Magnum when
the safety's off. Principle with me which I recommend
to all Righters of Wrongs who prefer being alive to
dead. Hickory's standing just about three feet to my
left when Tate turns and moves toward the bedroom,
and that's the moment when I make my move. I drop
behind old Hick and give him my best clip in the back
so he lunges forward, throws his arms up in the air
like he was signaling touchdown, and bellows like a
picadored bull.

"Tate whirls around and unloads, but I'm crouched
down behind Hick and he takes the bullet in the solar
plexus, then falls backward on top of me. The recoil
backs Tate up some, he shot off with one hand only,
and it takes him a second to see what's happened.
'Lord, help me now!' I pray, and what do you think?
Faster than Federal Express he sends an Irish angel to
my rescue."

Ahmad took a long draught of his brandy.

"Know what, J. D.?" he said. "This more or less
balances our books again. We're even."

The buzzer from the viewing lobby rasped, and I
got up, moved to the door, and snapped on the viewing
screen. Jim Squires's square face loomed mistily into
view. I pressed the entrance button, then opened the
door and waited by the elevator. Ahmad stood behind
me, his brandy glass still in hand.

"You know," I said, "Jim's not going to like this
scene. It will remind him of how he met you."

"Shouldn't shock him too much. Just an old déjà
vu," Ahmad said.

The rest was routine. Lieutenant Halberstein from
Troy's homicide section arrived a few minutes later,
just after the EMS paramedic pronounced Hickory

dead. We made our statements in the kitchen, sipping another brandy.

The next day, Terry and Mrs. Garfinkel—none other than receptionist Nanette, Tattersby's only child—were arrested, and Terry talked. The Beef House was perhaps the largest cocaine distribution center for sophisticated users in the entire northwest area of metropolitan Detroit. Its method was simple. A dinner reservation was made for reliable customers, who authorized the use of their credit cards for their small drug purchases listed under various labels—tobaccos, jewelry, option, future, dinner party catering, case of expensive wine—payable to SMACO. Of course, the customer had a meal, but always he took home a doggy bag of leftover steak, veal, whatever—and in the bag, which was always delivered by Willie, the head busboy, was a packet of white whiz. On the way out, the customer signed the credit authorization that Nanette had ready for him at the reception desk.

Willie Tattersby had come on Harry Jenkins when he was prowling around the basement, just as I had done. Harry was standing in front of the padlocked freezer when Willie had whacked him in the neck with the crowbar, Terry testified. Willie hauled him into the meat storage unit, turned down the temperature, and later Tiny Tim and Janescu had packed Harry into the trunk of Rick Janescu's car, just as I had been packed into the trunk of Hickory's Lincoln town car. There was one difference, however: Harry was dead.

Janescu was rearraigned on a charge of conspiring to conceal a murder, and received a three- to five-year sentence. There were other charges against Tiny Tim, and he went up for eight to fifteen years. Nanette was not indicted—there was no one to testify against her except her husband, who couldn't, and her father, who declined to do so. Willie, a Canadian citizen whose home was a fancy condominium on Riverside Drive in

Windsor, apparently ran the cocaine from a Canadian connection, and after a prompt extradition, he was given two life sentences. Lawyers' fees, I have no doubt, consumed whatever assets were left in the accounts of the Southeastern Michigan Assets Company.

Emmett Harvey knew nothing of the drug operation, and I saw no reason to involve him. Neither did Willie, figuring no doubt that there was little to be gained by confessing to any more crimes than he was already charged with. I had a talk with Charlotte and Emmett a few days after things had settled down.

"You can both forget about the Colorado Beef House," I told them. "People there were involved in distributing drugs, but the guilty parties have been arrested and the place is padlocked. They gave you a mickey, Emmett, at that poker game, then planted Cindy Schumac's strangled body alongside your bed so they could blackmail you into handling their phony stock accounts.

"I have two pieces of advice for you, Emmett. Trust your wife in the future. Don't play the machismo game of protecting her from your own follies. She loves you and she's got a brain. The least you can do is give her the respect of confiding in her if you get in trouble."

He agreed, nodding his head vigorously and squeezing Charlotte's hand. The expression in Charlotte's eyes as, looking at me, she responded to Emmett's hand-squeeze, almost—but not quite—made the risks I had run on her account seem worthwhile.

"What's the other piece of advice?" Emmett asked.

"An old truism. Never play poker with strangers," I said, to which Emmett replied, "Amen!"

"Does Liz know?" Charlotte asked as I was leaving. "Did you tell her anything?"

"Oh, no."

"Then she doesn't know and doesn't have to," I said. "I'll tell her when I give her my bill that it was an irregularity in the office accounts that I managed to straighten out, that everything now is lovey-dovey between you two. Okay?"

I invited the doctor to meet Ahmad and me at Moffat's one Saturday afternoon for lunch. I explained that Ahmad worked with me, that he was an expert computer accountant, and that his labors had been vital in discovering the statistical errors that had found their way into the computer and had been driving Emmett Harvey up the wall. He would have to be paid at the same rate as me. We settled for ten thousand dollars, five of which Ahmad and I had previously agreed to give to Milly Jenkins.

Dr. Mansfield wrote a check on the spot, and paid for our lunch. But just before she left us, she said, "Do you remember our first meeting here, Miss Mulroy?"

"Of course."

"I tried to lie to you, but I wasn't successful, was I?"

"That's right."

"It's difficult for honest professional people to lie successfully, don't you agree?"

I smiled. She smiled. Ahmad didn't smile.

Then Dr. Mansfield went away, happy because now she had no delicately personal matters to worry her.

Epilogue

Three days before Christmas I received a telephone call, and I recognized the genteel voice of Nathan immediately. The Janescu hearings were over—Janescu pleaded guilty, and had already received his sentence, but was being held in Pontiac's jail as a witness vital to the prosecution's case against Tattersby, scheduled to go to trial in early February.

"I was wondering, Miss Mulroy, whether we might have lunch together tomorrow," Nathan said. "I should like to discuss the Lanzetti necklace with you—if you're still interested in it."

"That would be nice," I said. "Mr. Hickory certainly will have no use for it, wherever he may be."

"Quite. You live in Birmingham, I in Grosse Pointe Woods. May I suggest a restaurant halfway between our homes?"

"Do."

"Brock's Seafood Grotto then. It's a relatively new place that has an excellent fish menu and quality German wines purchasable by the glass. On Maple Road just past Mound."

"I'll find it."

"Twelve-fifteen then?"

"Twelve-fifteen."

I was really flush—for me. I had the better part of the twenty-five hundred that was my share of Dr. Mansfield's fee, and ten thousand of the twenty I had earned solving our last case, the Winkler problem (the other ten, at Ed's insistence, I had invested in a municipal bond mutual fund). As I drove along Maple looking for Brock's Seafood Grotto, I was wondering how flexible Nathan's price might be. He had asked forty-eight hundred when he had shown the necklace to Ed and me at our initial meeting, though he insisted a proper retail price would be nearer six thousand. I believed him, but it would be foolish not to check with Art Spring before I bought it.

The Grotto was set back from Maple in the rear of a small intersection shopping mall, anchored by a Farmer Jack supermarket at one end and a Frank's Nursery Products shop at the other. The menu in the window was expensive enough, so I concluded the food must be of better than average quality. I hesitated in the dark of the subdued lighting inside, adjusting my eyes, and Nathan, who must have been waiting for me just inside the entrance, got to me before the hostess. He carried his case in his right hand.

"I like prompt people, Jane," he said smiling. "Promptness indicates respect for other people. I have a table for two just under a wall lamp."

The waitresses here were middle-aged and wore black chiffon dresses and aprons with a ruffled edging. They were professional waitresses. I ordered a glass of a Bernkastle riesling, Nathan a small pot of decaf.

"I have been following the newspaper stories about the Colorado Beef House murders and drug scandal very carefully," he said. "I am given to understand that you were instrumental in bringing those villains to account."

Neither my name nor Ahmad's had appeared in the newspapers, our role in the developments being accounted for by the generic term "investigators." "Investigators" discovered this, that, and some other matters. Of course, Nathan had known many people who had frequented the Beef House, all of the girls, so I supposed that Lorelei, Nina, or even Nanette had told him that I had been involved.

"I had a little to do with it," I confessed. "A very small role."

"You dissemble well," he commented. "I am glad to see Will Tattersby finally come to justice."

"You knew he was dispensing drugs?"

"No, but I knew he was into some kind of illegal mischief. Had I known it was drugs, I should probably have gone to the police."

"Probably?"

The waitress, who did not give us her name or show us her bosom, interrupted our conversation. I was hungry, and ordered a tuna steak with broccoli hollandaise, and Nathan ordered an omelette quiche. The food was excellent, and the wine good enough to tempt me into a second, very large bell-shaped glass.

Finally, after our table had been cleared, as I sipped my wine and Nathan his second cup of decaf, he lifted his case from the floor, set it on the table, and opened it. He withdrew the Lanzetti necklace, and placed it in front of me on a dark velveteen cloth. In the dim light it glowed with true gold luster, and I knew I was going to buy it.

"I sense that you are still interested, Jane," Nathan said.

"It's very beautiful, it grows on you, and I do want it. If I can afford it," I answered, knowing that I would pay his price if it came to that.

"Do you have a dollar?" he asked.

I figured that he wanted a little extra change to tip the waitress, and I gave him a dollar that should have been retired by the last two bank tellers who had handled it. He drew a slip of form-printed paper from a pocket in the multi-pocketed case and began writing on it. After he had studied what he had written, he handed it to me.

"Your receipt," he said. "All sales are final."

"This is to acknowledge the receipt from *Jane D. Mulroy* the sum of *One Dollar* ($1.00) in full payment for *One Gold Necklace by Dante Lanzetti.*"

I couldn't believe what I was reading, but Nathan's yellow-toothed smile told me he wasn't joking.

"Why?" I asked.

"The signature will tell you."

The signature? *Nathan Garfinkel* it read.

"Terry is my only son," Nathan explained. "You have freed him from a pit of vipers, and now, after his divorce, he can become the man his father-in-law and his wife prevented him from being. I thank you in the only way an old man like me can. If I could do more for you, I would."

I reached across the table and we held hands for a minute or two. His eyes were clouded with tears. Neighboring patrons took notice.

Ever the gentleman, Nathan saw me to my car.

With the necklace in my purse in a velvet bag, I drove home slowly. The streets seemed cleaner, the air purer, because if not everything, at least some things were right with the world. But as I pulled into the dark of my apartment's underground garage, a complicating thought darkened my mood. It must have taken me all of two seconds to dispel it. Damned if I was going to share the necklace with Ahmad! He already has *two* gold chains.